# C, My
# Name is
# Cal

## Also by NORMA FOX MAZER:

*A, My Name Is Ami*
*B, My Name Is Bunny*
*D, My Name Is Danita*
*E, My Name Is Emily*
*Three Sisters*
*When We First Met*

# Norma Fox Mazer

# C, My Name is Cal

AN
**APPLE**
PAPERBACK

SCHOLASTIC INC.
New York Toronto London Auckland Sydney

No part of this publication may be reproduced in whole or in part, or stored in a retrieval system, or transmitted in any form or by any means, electronic, mechanical, photocopying, recording, or otherwise, without written permission of the publisher. For information regarding permission, write to Scholastic Inc., 730 Broadway, New York, NY 10003.

ISBN 0-590-41832-7

12 11 10 9 8 7 6 5 4 3 2 1    11    1 2 3 4 5 6/9

Printed in the U.S.A.    28

*For Joan Stanley and
the Book Club kids
at Arcade*

# C, My
# Name is
# Cal

# Chapter 1

Garo and I live together. Or maybe I should say I and my mother live in Garo's house — or to be even more exact, in Garo's and his father's house. Garo's father is a pilot. He'll come home for a day, two days, three days at most, then get a call and off he goes. He's always on standby.

Alan must have gotten his call for work in the middle of the night, because when Garo woke up this morning, he found three twenty-dollar bills under his pillow. "Look at this, Cal," he said. "Look what Dad left me." He yawned. "We're rich."

"Uh-uh," I said. "You're rich."

When Mom and I first moved into Garo's house, I started making up this story in my head that my father was on standby, too. That while Mom and I had been moving from cheap place to cheaper place, my father had been busy, also. That he wasn't just *gone*. No. He'd been going to pilot school, putting in those flying hours, and one of these days he'd show up again.

Or maybe he'd call first. "Cal? Coming to see you any moment now. I'm on standby, son; it keeps me busy." Back then I could still "hear" my father's voice in my head. But now it's nearly nine years that I haven't heard his voice, and I can't remember it at all.

I don't know what he looks like, either. I mean, I have a photo of him, and that's what I "remember." A tall, skinny man wearing a blue sport jacket.

"The money's for both of us," Garo said. "What'll we do with it?" Money bores him. He's careless with it. He never knows how much he has. Not me. I always know what I have, and it's never enough.

Mom gives me money sometimes, but mostly when she has anything extra, she puts it in my college savings account. One of the reasons she took this job was that we got room and board, which meant she could save money.

Once, before we got to be friends, Garo said to me, "Cal, I just got it. I just got that you and Nina don't have money. You don't even have your own home."

"So what, stupid?" I said. "What's the big revelation?"

4

He gave me an uncomfortable smile. "I just meant — "

"I know what you just meant. Shut up." As I said it, I thought that I could never be someone who had to deal with people or the public. I didn't know how to be tactful. I didn't know how to say things nicely. I could never be a salesman, which is what my father is. Or was, nine years ago. And still is, for all I know. Not that I care. It doesn't matter to me what he does. In all this time, he's never come to see me, he's never called. All he's ever done is send me three picture postcards, each one from a different place.

When the first card came from Arkansas, about two months after we moved in with Garo and his father, Mom said, "Now how in the world did Cameron Miller know where we are?" I had to remind her that even though my father had been roaming, we two still lived in the same town and the same state. And even though we lived in the Vitullis' house, we had our own phone and a separate listing in the phone book, under Mom's name.

The second postcard was mailed from Florida. It had a picture of flamingos on it. I got it four years ago, after my ninth birthday. I think it was supposed to be a birthday card. It said, GOOD LUCK, SON! LOVE, DAD. Then it had a P.S. MAYBE SEE YOU ONE OF THESE DAYS. When my mother read it, she said, "Well, don't hold your breath."

The last postcard came two Christmases ago, from a town called Newbridge, in Maine. It said, DEAR CALVIN, PRETTY COUNTRY OUT HERE. VERY QUIET AND COLD. I HOPE LIFE IS GOING OKAY FOR YOU. LOVE, DAD.

Garo rolled up one of the twenties and flipped it across to me. "I owe you ten more." He was still in his striped pajamas.

"You don't owe me anything." I tossed it back. "Your money," I said. "Not mine." I pulled on my jeans and thought how sometimes I hated everything in this house — the chairs, the curtains, the rugs, even the toilets. None of it was Mom's and mine.

"What's your problem, boy?" Garo threw the money at me again. When he gets excited, his freckles blaze up. His entire face is covered with freckles. So are his arms and legs. "Take it, Cal. Take it!"

"Forget it, boy. I don't want your damn money." I wadded the bill and threw it in the wastebasket.

"You're so bleeping stubborn, Cal." Garo's always polite, even when he's mad.

"And you don't understand anything." I went down the stairs. Garo ran after me. Mom was in the kitchen, cooking breakfast. "Mom," I said, "tell Garo I don't want his bleeping money."

"His *bleeping* money?" Mom said. She pinched my cheek. "What kind of funny talk is that?"

Then to Garo, she said, "We've been through this before, hon. But I'll remind you again that

6

I am an employee in this house, and Calvin is the son of the employee. And your money is your money."

"Nina — " Garo sat down at the table and put his head in his hands.

"Not his money. Yours. Is that clear? Should I say it again? Calvin is the employee's son, not the son of the employer. Do you read my meaning? Money given you by your father is yours. Not Calvin's."

"I hate to hear this, Nina," Garo said.

I started to feel sorry for Garo. When Mom gets going, it's like she grabs you by the ear with her voice. "Is that clear?" I said in my mother's top sergeant voice. I pounded him on the back in a friendly manner.

Garo swiveled around and butted me in the stomach. I grabbed him by the hair, and he locked his arms around my waist. It was an impasse. Garo is almost half a year older than me, but smaller and less developed. He's inches shorter and built like a football. I'm built more like a stick, but I've got body hair, and my voice has changed. Another thing about us is that Garo doesn't just look younger than me, he acts younger. This is just the truth; I'm not boasting or anything.

"Breakfast is ready, you two," Mom said. We broke apart. Mom's in charge here. She's the housekeeper or house mother or house administrator or Major General Discipliner. Whatever you want to call her. Garo's father has tried on all those titles for Mom at one time or another. Mom says, "I don't care what Alan calls me, as long as he pays the bills and my salary."

That's Mom being witty. In fact, she does care what she's called. For instance, Garo can't call her Mom. He went through a stage where he wanted to, but she wouldn't allow it. She was firm. "I like everything clear," she said. "And it's clear, Garo, that I'm not your mom. You can call me Nina."

So with whatever else Garo has, house and father and money, at least I have that. Mom is my mom.

We sat down to eat breakfast. The stuff on the stove that my mother was stirring turned out to be something called Bircher Muesli. It looked just about as bad as it sounded. "What is this stuff?" I said. I'm finicky about food.

"Cereal," my mother said. "Put some milk on it, brown sugar; it'll warm your gut for the cold walk to school."

I read the box. FLAX, WHOLE WHEAT, RICE BRAN, WALNUTS, ALMONDS, RAISINS, PINEAPPLE, AND OTHER WHOLE GRAINS AND FRUIT. "Where's the fruit?" I said, poking around with my spoon.

"It looks like snot to me," Garo said. But he was already shoveling the snively stuff in. Nothing bothers his appetite.

"You say that word about good food?" Mom said.

Garo and I both looked at her in surprise. A word like snot ordinarily doesn't bother Mom. She's not the type to mind a few rough words. She once ate fish eyes to find out what they tasted like. Another time, on a dare, she ate a live ant. "Damn thing was crunchy, and wooo!, was it sour," she said.

"Who dared you to do it?" I asked her.

"Oh, someone. No one you ever knew." She laughed, and I got the idea, which I'd never had before, that she'd had a whole life before me, a life I didn't know about. That was strange.

"I hate this bircher stuff," I said.

"Cal, you like it," Mom informed me. "I got a special on it. Don't start my day off wrong by telling me I wasted money."

"Are you tired, Nina?" Garo asked kind of sweetly.

"No."

"Got something on your mind?"

"My mind is a total blank, hon. Shut up and eat." Suddenly she started laughing and laughed so hard she had to sit down. Garo started laughing, too. I looked from him to her. Sometimes it seems like he's more on Mom's wavelength, more like her than I am. Maybe they were mother and son in another life. They both think the world is fairly amusing. They're kind of jolly. They get mad fast and get right over it and laugh. They even look a little alike, both short and overweight.

9

I suppose I'm like my father, Cameron Miller. My mother says he is — or was, when he was around us — a tall, glum, broody man. I know I'm tall. I think I'm sort of broody. I hope I'm not too glum.

# Chapter 2

When Mom and I first moved in with Garo and Alan, I was seven and not happy about the move. I didn't like living in someone else's house. I didn't like Alan. When I saw him in his blue pilot's uniform, he looked like a policeman to me. I thought that somehow he knew all the wrong things I'd done. I figured there were a lot of them. I lied sometimes. I didn't do what my mom wanted. I hated my father, and I was still babyish, secretly sleeping with Opha Kangaroo every night. And the worst of it was that I shunned his son, Garo. I hated Garo, too. I didn't like that my mother was nice to him.

I suppose I was scared, even panicked, afraid of what was going to happen next. So many things had already happened to me. Mom and my father were divorced when I was five. My father took off. My mother wouldn't talk about him. She didn't even like to hear his name, Miller, which was also her name and my name. She kept trying to find the right job, so I wouldn't have to have baby-sitters. And we moved from apartment to apartment. Until we landed ourselves with Garo and Alan.

In the beginning, Garo wasn't that friendly himself. His mother had died the year before, and various people had been taking care of him, and he was sick of it. And he didn't know what to make of gloomy, skinny me. He was shorter, rounder, softer. We were just different.

We lived in the same house and we weren't friends. We didn't fight particularly, we just avoided each other. I was a loner; at least I thought I was. I didn't think I needed friends. Or maybe I didn't want them, didn't want anyone to know I didn't have a father or a home of my own.

But the year Garo was kept back in fourth grade, things changed. He was five months older than me, and he had been a grade ahead of me. But then he wasn't passed, because he wasn't reading well enough.

If that had been me, Mom would have gone up in steam and smoke. She would have torn me apart and told me I was letting my brains turn to mush. She couldn't do that to Garo, naturally, but she tried to get Alan to whip him into shape. I don't mean actually *whip*, of course. Mom's idea of whipping is to pep talk you to death.

Alan tried. He talked seriously to Garo, his voice coming from deep in his throat. Rumble rumble rumble. But then he was gone, and when he came back it was rumble rumble again. Wherever you were in the house, you could hear that rumble rumble rumble. Garo listened politely. He listened politely when Mom talked to him, too. But nothing anyone said made an impression on him, and for one reason. He didn't think he needed to be a good reader.

"I know what I want to be when I grow up," he said. "I'm going to be a talk show host. I won't be one of those sarcastic guys who yell at everyone who calls in. I'm going to be one of those guys who are wise and smart and help other people solve their problems."

"Where are you getting all this wisdom?" I said. "I don't see any signs of it yet." I thought he was a real dope not to know it was important to know how to read.

"I'll learn from experience."

"What if people write you letters when you're a talk show host? They're going to do that. They're not just going to call in. How are you going to read their letters?"

Garo's mouth fell open. Then he said quickly, "I'll get someone to read them for me."

"What if you have to make a contract?" I got that idea from Mom's contract with Alan. When she took the job, she said even though she knew it had to be a 24-hour-a-day, seven-day-a-week job because of Garo, she still had some rights, and she wanted them in writing. That's why the attic is ours and off limits to Garo and Alan. And that's why we have our own phone and our own listing in the phone book.

"I'll hire people. A lawyer," Garo said.

"What if they cheat you? What if they don't read you the contract right?" I stumped him again. "You won't even know what's in it for yourself."

"I'll hire honest people."

He had an answer for everything. "Oh, I give up," I said. What did I care anyway?

It was Mom's idea to have Garo and me read together at night. "Why me?" I said. I didn't want to spend all that time with him.

"If you don't do it, Cal, I'll have to," Mom said. She gave me a little light slap on the face. "You might as well pull your weight here, hon."

So every night after supper, Garo and I sat down at the dining room table and took turns reading out loud to each other. Remember, this was before I liked him. So it wasn't something I looked forward to.

Actually, it wasn't that bad, because I like reading. I might even love it. When it was my turn to read, I didn't mind at all. I could just forget Garo was there. But when it was his turn, it was torture listening to him stumble through a page.

"Relax!" I said. I punched him.

"Hey!"

"That's to help you relax." I punched him again. He punched me back. "That's the idea," I said. "Don't you feel better now?"

"No."

"Well, maybe this will do it." I gave him another knock, and he hit me over the head with the book.

Mom came in. "Settle down and read, you two."

"Yes, ma'am," Garo said, and kicked me under the table.

It was somewhere in there that we got to like each other. And Garo even learned to read better.

In the morning, Garo couldn't find his red socks, so he wore mine to school. He's particular about the things he wears. Today he wanted red socks and nothing else would do.

"Why red?" I said, when we went out. I looked down at my feet and saw that somehow I'd put on two different colored socks. My left foot was green, my right foot was blue.

"It's Valentine's Day," Garo said. He bounds when he walks, he bounces. His personality is cheerful, and even the way he walks is cheerful. "I need good luck. Red luck. Red for hearts, red for love."

"Red for blood and gore," I said. It had snowed overnight, and I pulled my scarf around my neck.

"I want valentines, Cal," he said. "Lots of valentines. Do you think I'll get them?"

"Who cares, Garo! We're too old for that stuff."

I was never crazy and wild about girls the way

Garo has always been. I used to think something was wrong with me, because he liked girls so much more than I did. Right from second grade on, he's been romantic and in love with someone or other.

I can't remember feelings like that from so young. Except for one teacher, Mrs. Eisenor. I used to sit and stare at her arms. She always wore sleeveless blouses, and her arms were big and fresh-looking.

Around fourth grade, I really started liking the girls in my class, but I didn't talk about it — or show it, either, I guess. I had my feelings, but I kept them all inside.

Garo shoved against me. "You'll get valentines. You get them every year; the girls all give you valentines. Smoochy, smoochy!"

I packed a snowball, took aim. "Garo, my boy — " The snowball smacked into a tree. "I don't care, one way or the other. That stuff is for elementary school."

"No, the girls are still doing valentines." He put his puppy dog face in mine. "This is the day you find out if girls like you. I know what you'll find out, but I'm afraid what I'll find out. I'm telling you, Cal, today might be very detrimental to my mental health."

"Who is it that you want to get a valentine from, anyway? You have some particular girl in mind?"

He changed the subject. "Remember Valentine's Day in grade school? Remember third grade? Remember Jeanne Foster? The worst day of my life!"

"She was the one with buck teeth, wasn't she?"

"She did not have buck teeth."

"Sure, she did. Did she send you a valentine?"

"I wanted her to. I was positive she would. She told me out on the playground that she was going to send me a valentine. I waited all day. I kept thinking she was going to give it to me in private. It was like waiting to be picked for the softball team in gym and never being picked."

"Garo, you're always picked for the team."

"It's only true when you're there."

"Garo, you're crazy as a coot."

"No, it's the truth. When you're there, Cal, they pick me. When you're not there, they go right over me."

Garo has a way of building me up beyond what I really am. He asks me questions and then waits for my answers, as if I've got all the right ones. Once he asked, "Cal, how many toes are there in the world?"

He was serious, I think. Or maybe it was a joke I didn't get. That's possible. Actually, it's an easy question if you know the world population, except that the population is changing instantly, constantly. I once saw a display in a store window showing X billions of people in the world. The last number flipped without stopping. *Bip bip bip bip bip bip bip bip bipbipbipbipbip-*

*bipbip* . . . While I stood there, 650 people were added to the world. It was sort of frightening. The world doesn't get any bigger, but every second more people are pressing in on it.

The way Garo looks up to me makes me uneasy. I'm not that smart. I don't do anything special. I'm not a sports genius. I'm not good with music. I'm not scientific. OK, I'm good in school, but so what? I like to read and I remember things, which is why I like studying, but it's not as if I'm forcing myself to do something I don't enjoy.

Maybe I like school because Mom's father was a school principal in Chicago. My grandmother died a long time ago, and my grandfather lives alone. Mom says he's not a happy man, and she never got along with him. "He didn't want me to marry your father, who had no special education."

Considering the way things worked out with my father doing his disappearing act, maybe my grandfather knew something. I asked Mom once if we'd ever visit him. "No," she said. "N. O. If that man doesn't want to know he's got a grandson, then I don't want to know him."

"Do you know Leslie Branch likes you, Cal?" Garo said.

"Get lost. She does not. Where'd you hear that?" Leslie Branch has thin red lips and a sharp nose. She's cute, like a tall witch would be cute. She flashes her eyes.

"She told me herself. She said she wished she could kiss you."

"I heard that she likes everything in pants." I'd also heard that she kept a record book, with the ambition to kiss every boy in our class and then get it into the *Guinness Book of World Records*.

"She kissed me," Garo said happily.

This was news. I'd never thought much about Leslie before, but now I felt jealousy. "When did this happen?"

"The other day in gym, I mean, after gym. On the stairs going down to the locker rooms."

"A real kiss?"

"It wasn't a sock in the mouth."

I'd had party kisses, but not the real thing. "What was it like?"

"Oooh, soft, and —" He began weaving around with a crazy smile, hugging himself, acting dopey. He fell down in a bank of snow. "Oh, boy, Cal, oh, boy!"

"She kissed you on the lips or the cheek?" I asked.

"On the lips. Smackola!" Garo rubbed his mouth. His freckles stood out. "She kissed me, but I think — you know what I think? She really wanted to kiss you. That's why she kissed me."

"That makes sense," I said.

"Well, she told me — she said she wanted you to kiss her, and I should tell you. So I think she kissed me like a bribe. Get it? So I'd tell you, and you'd do it. You know, now I'm sort of a walking advertisement for her kiss. This is good stuff, Cal. It'll be a real experience for you."

I started thinking about it and I got excited, but I didn't like to show it, so I grunted.

"Will you do it? Will you kiss her?" Garo asked.

"Not if she's the one you want a valentine from." It was a shot in the dark.

"No, it's not Leslie! You can kiss Leslie as much as you want. The one I want is — " He cut himself off. "No, I can't tell. She isn't even looking at me. Not that way." He slapped himself in the face. "I'm getting depressed," he moaned.

"Garo, you're getting depressed over nothing, man. Whoever she is, she's going to send you a valentine. I have a feeling."

He looked at me. "Really?"

"Yeah, really," I bluffed.

"Okay," he said.

Okay? One word from me and everything is fine? Why does he do that? Why does he let me say bull and get away with it? I was just saying the first thing that popped into my head, trying to calm him down.

"Knock, knock, Cal," he said.

Garo and his jokes. They're usually bad. "Who's there?"

"Picasso."

"Picasso who?"

"Picass I have a song in my art."

"Picass I have a song in my art," I repeated. I didn't get it, but I made it sound like I was just being ironic and a little bored with Garo's basic-type humor. Then I got it. Picass I have a song in my 'art. Double joke. Picasso was a famous painter. "Funny," I said.

20

"Yeah, it's a good one." Garo bounded along-side me. He only gets worried, like about the valentines, sometimes, and then it blows right over. Sometimes if I'm a little glum, his cheerfulness gets on my nerves.

Once when he was babbling about Life and Happiness, I said, "Garo, your mother is dead. Is life perfect? No, it isn't."

"I know that." His freckles stood out as if he were going to cry. Garo can cry. I can't. I used to when I w~s really little, I can remember crying into Opha Kangaroo's fur pocket. But then I stopped. I stopped myself when I was ten years old. I felt ashamed that I cried. I felt mad at myself every time I cried. So I stopped.

But I've heard Garo cry lots of times, even now that he's fourteen, mostly from thinking about his mother. It was mean of me to bring it up like that. But as fast as he admitted that life could never be perfect, he added, "But it's almost perfect. I've got you and Nina and my father. And even my father's job is perfect."

Which was sort of a family joke, something Mom, Garo, and I agreed on a long time ago. Not because Alan is a pilot and Garo can fly anywhere he wants for free, which he can. But because Alan is a fanatic about a clean house and rules and quiet and anything else you can be a fanatic about. Fortunately for all of us, he has a job that keeps him away from home most of the time.

When he does come home between flights, we all get a little tense. He has a way of running his finger over shelves you'd never think about otherwise, and looking for things that are out of place and pointing this stuff out to Mom. Maybe it's a good quality in a pilot — I mean, being so meticulous. He probably would never do anything careless that might hurt the passengers on his plane.

Usually Mom laughs at him, but sometimes it gets to her. I remember once Alan found dust in some closet or other and called her to see. She blew up. She screamed, "Mr. Vitulli! Do you want a dust-free house, is that your main concern, or is your son your main concern?"

She sent Garo and me out of the house, but we didn't miss a thing. It was summer and all the windows were open.

"I'm doing my best," Mom yelled, "to take care of your boy, and if my best isn't good enough for you, fire me."

That scared me. If she quit Alan, where would we go? Where would we live? How would Mom make money for us?

"I'll find someplace else to work, Mr. Vitulli. I didn't get fat on this job. I've always been this way!"

Garo's freckles were so bright he looked like a speckled egg. "She doesn't mean it," I said. But I didn't know. I wasn't sure, but I had to say something to Garo. He looked ready to puke.

"Mrs. Nina, calm down," Alan was saying in his deep, soothing Captain of the Ship voice. "Mrs. Nina, I certainly didn't mean to imply that you're not doing a superior job. Mrs. Nina! Mrs.

Nina, are you calm now? Is it okay? Is it okay?"

Alan calls Mom Mrs. Nina, because when we first came here, she said she definitely didn't want him calling her Nina. "Too familiar." And she even more definitely didn't want to be called Mrs. Miller. "I do not like being reminded that that is my legal name," she said.

So she's Mom to me, Mrs. Nina to Alan, and Nina to Garo. And Garo's father is Mr. Vitulli to Mom, Dad to Garo, and Alan to me — or sometimes Captain, if I sense he's in an especially friendly mood.

# Chapter 3

"Hi-i-i, Garo! How are you, cutie?" Leslie Branch shoved into the signing line ahead of Garo. Dave Ramsey, an author, had come to our school to talk to us. We were lined up in the library so he could sign our books. I had one he wrote called *Secret of the White Roof*. I'd read it three times and brought it from home. Garo had a Ramsey book called *If I Die . . .* He'd bought it this morning, because it was the skinniest one for sale. Garo still wasn't a great reader.

"You don't mind me cutting in, do you, hon?" Leslie gave me a flashing glance, but it was Garo she spoke to. She was wearing a pink sweater with rabbits around the border. She kept patting Garo on the head. "Curly curls," she said.

Garo blushed, his freckles seemed to melt all over his face. Was he thinking about her kissing

24

him? The girls think it's cute when Garo blushes. They tease him and shove him around. They like him. I told him it was foolish for him to worry about valentine cards, and I was right. He got plenty! I got a few myself, including one from Leslie with her lipsticked mouth print on it.

"I heard this book is really creepy," Garo said to Leslie. On the cover, it showed a skull sort of hovering mistily in the air, and a boy hiding behind a tree.

"Are you going to read it?" she asked. She looked over at me again.

I acted like I didn't notice.

"Sure I'll read it," Garo said. "I'll probably read it tonight." He jerked his thumb at me. "And this guy will read three books tonight."

"Shut up," I muttered, looking away.

"I want Mr. Ramsey's signature," Garo went on. "Someday it might be worth a lot of money. . . . Got your pen, Cal?" He held up his pen. "See this," he said to Leslie. "That's his mom." The pen had NINA MILLER, ASSISTANT TO CUB SCOUT TROOP 19, EAST DRUMLINS imprinted in gold. That was from way back when Garo and I went through our Cub Scout phase. We were selling embossed pens to raise money. Mom had ordered four dozen.

After Mr. Ramsey autographed her book, Leslie Branch stopped by me. "Want to sign my book, too?"

"I'm not an author."

"I just thought you might like to." I thought

it was a pretty dumb thing to do, but I took her book and wrote my name in it. Then I drew a skull and crossbones under it.

"What's that for?" Leslie asked.

I shrugged. "Poison."

"You're poison?" She gave me a big smile. "I drink poison every Saturday night."

Just as Leslie left, Fern Light and her skinny friend, Angel Hayes, pulled the same stunt on Garo and pushed into the line ahead of him. All the pushy girls in school know Garo. He didn't mind. He just started telling me a joke in a loud voice.

"What did the man who jumped off the Empire State Building say as he went past the thirty-sixth floor?"

Fern Light turned and looked at him with raised eyebrows.

"So far . . ." Garo broke up laughing. "So far . . . so good!"

"That is a very low form of humor," Fern said. She has thick dark eyebrows and really big, slightly bulging dark eyes. She has definite opinions about everything and makes sure everyone knows them. Angel Hayes, on the other hand, hardly ever says anything. She's Fern's devoted follower. She's got a little mole on the corner of her lip, which was twitching almost as fast as Fern's eyebrows were wagging.

I think those wagging eyebrows made Garo a little crazy. He started telling another bad joke in the same loud voice. "What did the man say when he was asked if the basement was damp?"

"Shut up," I said.

"Why, that place is so dry down there, the bugs die of thirst."

"Oh, lord," Fern said. She stepped up to the table where Dave Ramsey was sitting. "Hello, Mr. Ramsey! Thank you for being here. Would you please sign this book for Iris? That's spelled I. R. I. S."

"Certainly," Dave Ramsey said. He bent over the book. He had a bald spot on top of his head.

"Iris is not your name," Garo said.

Fern turned around. The eyebrows started wagging. "Oh, thank you for informing me, Garo! Oh, heavens, if you hadn't let me know, saved me in the nick of time, BIG identity crisis!" Next to her, Angel Hayes's mole was smiling.

I socked Garo on the arm. "Hey," he said feebly. He stared after Fern as she left, with that puppy dog look on his face. That's when I finally got it. Fern was the girl he'd been hoping would send him a valentine. She didn't.

"Hey," I said, and socked him again. "Cheer up."

Then the author looked up. "Well, boys, how do you want me to sign your books?"

Garo put his book down on the table. "Write, 'For my good friend, Garretson Vitulli.' "

Garo hung around with me at basketball practice. He handed the ball off to me, below the basket. On the way home, he said, "If I ever grow enough, I'll make the team."

"Garo, you say that as if it's your height, I mean your *lack* of height, that kept you off the team."

"Well, it did."

"No. You've got a nice jump shot. You know what Coach said. You didn't take the game seriously, you joked around too much."

"I'm too short," he said.

"Look at Paxson on the Bulls. Look at Price. Look at Jackson. All little guys — and all great players." I sounded slick, self-confident, like I knew all the answers. Who was I to talk about Garo's lack of concentration? I'm not that great, I'm not great at all. I was one of the last picks for the team. The best thing I can say about myself is that I really like the game. I could run the ball up and down the court all day. And then turn and leap, like I'm Michael Jordan.

And I like the game, too, because when you're playing basketball, you can't think of anything else. Nothing but basketball. And that's good, because there are times when I can't stop thinking about things — like my father. Like, where is he? And why hasn't he ever come to see me? And what would he think of me?

I wonder if he'd like to see me play. Every game, at some point, the thought flashes through my mind that he's in the stands, watching. I think it helps my game. But then other times, I wonder, Does he hate me? Does he think anything of me? I get all these questions rushing around in my brain, sort of like mice in a cage. And then I think about what I'll do when I get out of school, and that makes me crazy, too, because everything is a question. And I don't have any of the answers.

# Chapter 4

Mom was on the phone with Tom Lustig when Garo and I came back home. I could tell who it was from the way she turned her back and said, "Well, I better get off now . . . the endless appetites are here." Then she listened. Tom is a big talker. I suppose he's her boyfriend. She never says it. She says, "My friend Tom." My friend Tom is a commercial photographer. My friend Tom takes pictures to put on the boxes products come in. You see that toaster box with that picture of a happy smiling woman taking toast out of her wonderful XYZ toaster? My friend Tom took that picture.

Mom posed for one of Tom's pictures once for a weight loss product called Wate Pow(d)er. It showed her with her head tipped back, drinking a Wate Pow(d)er Cocktail.

"Your Aunt Shirley called today," Mom said to Garo after she hung up.

"What does she want?"

"Don't know, hon. She wants you to call her back."

"Do I have to? Calling California's expensive."

"Yeah, yeah," Mom said. "I know how much you worry about the phone bill. I told your aunt you'd call."

"What do you bet she wants me to come visit again?" Garo made a face.

He was right. Friday after school Mom and I drove him to the airport to get the plane to Los Angeles. Garo can fly any time he wants to. He'd flown out to Los Angeles just a few months ago to visit his Aunt Shirley. She's his father's sister.

It's always different for me at home when Garo's away. Mom has more time, and we do more things together. We went to the movies Friday night, Saturday we had lunch at Ground Round and went shopping, and that night we stayed up late watching an old Jimmy Cagney movie. It was fun being with Mom alone.

Garo called home Saturday and again on Sunday. He was coming home on Monday, but he couldn't wait to tell everything. "Cal, I ordered Mrs and Mr T with a Coke chaser on the plane. . . . We're driving down the coast to San Diego. And then maybe down to Mexico. Too bad you can't get on a plane and come out here, too. Cal in California." He cackled.

Even if Mom had the money, I wouldn't go out there. I've only flown once, and I didn't like it. I didn't like the feeling of being up in the air in this metal bird, this thing made by people who, let's face it, could be anything — stupid, lazy, careless, or just plain dumb. Something could happen. Something is always happening, isn't it?

Garo sounded so up in his phone calls that Mom and I didn't realize he was unhappy. But when he came home, the first thing he said was, "I hope I never go back there. My aunt said the only reason she invites me so much is that my father twists her arm."

"She said that?" Mom asked. Her voice rose.

Garo nodded. "She said me being there inconvenienced her a lot. She had to change all her plans. She said she only did it because it was her family duty."

Mom was furious. "Imagine telling a youngster that. I'm speaking to your father about this."

"Boy, am I glad to be home." Garo hung on Mom's arm, talking fast. They sat on the couch in the living room. It was a rainy day, and Mom had put a fire in the fireplace. "Cal, go make some popcorn," she said. I brought it back with sodas.

Garo was telling her everything, every last detail. The food he ate, every single meal, and every place he went with his aunt. Maybe she didn't want him there, but she did a lot of things with him. I was working on the popcorn. I didn't say anything. Words went through my head. *Fuzz head . . . fat slimy fink . . . sweaty fish slime-mouth . . . dopehead.* I walked out. I didn't want to hear my head. I didn't want to hear Garo. I didn't want to hear Mom cooing over him.

I went upstairs, to my real room, third floor, the one next to Mom's in the attic. Attic sounds like we're in the servants' quarters or something, but it's not that way. The attic is finished off with wood paneling, the bedrooms are big, and there's a private bath.

I don't use my room much anymore, since Garo and I started sharing down on the second floor. But if we have a fight, I always have someplace to go and be away from him. And then, sometimes, I just want to be away by myself, which is something Garo never understands.

I lay down on my bed and opened my book. When Mom called me for supper, I just kept on reading. I skipped supper, I skipped TV. Later, Mom came up and called me into her room. "Let's talk, my son." She patted the bed. "Sit."

"Arf arf." I sat down. But I didn't talk. I didn't have anything to say.

So she talked. She told me about when I was born, how happy she was to have me. She got out her envelope of pictures and showed me my baby pictures. I was never fat, even as a baby. There were a lot of pictures of me and her. "Do you have a picture of me and my father?"

"No."

"Didn't he ever want to have his picture taken with me?"

"I'm sorry, Cal, but I threw out every picture of him. I've told you that before."

I shrugged. "It doesn't matter."

"Never be jealous of Garo," she said.

"Who's jealous?"

"Just listen, Calvin. You have me. You always have me. That boy doesn't have a mother."

"I don't have a father," I said.

"It's not the same. And Garo doesn't have that much of a father, when it comes down to it," Mom said. "And don't you ever repeat that."

"I wouldn't," I said.

"I know you wouldn't," she said. "I can depend on you." She pinched my cheek, slapped it the way she does, lightly. Then she laughed and kissed me. "My boy," she said. And she kissed me again. And I felt sort of light-headed, happy, I guess, as if I could leap out the window and fly.

Garo came up to the attic later. He had his joke notebook under his arm. He keeps a record of jokes for the future. He says when he gets his job as a talk show host, he's going to be totally prepared. "What are you doing up here?" he said.

I held up my book.

"I started one, too," he said. "I read the first chapter."

"Congratulations. You going to read the second chapter?"

34

"Sure. I might even finish it. I'm going to use it for a book report."

"What book?"

"You know, the one the author guy signed."

"Dave Ramsey," I said. Garo never remembers names.

"Yeah, whatever. It's pretty good." He yawned. "Want to hear a joke?"

"Do I have a choice?"

"Sure, it's a free country."

"No, I'm not in the mood for a joke."

"How can you not be in the mood for a joke? A joke makes you laugh. Laughing makes you feel good. Feeling good is great."

I stared at him. "You know, Garo, everybody doesn't always want to feel good. Sometimes you just want to feel not so good."

"That's the way I feel when I can't remember my mother. Do you think it's bad I can't remember her?"

"No."

"Shouldn't I, though? I wasn't that young when she died. Six isn't that young."

"Why are you saying all this?"

"My aunt reminded me that the anniversary of my mother's death was coming. She asked me if I was feeling sad."

"Garo, I don't remember my father, and I don't think that's bad. Or sad, or glad, or anything. It's just the way it is."

"That's different. Your father's still around, Cal. I mean, he's alive."

"Maybe he is, and maybe he isn't. And if he is, I should remember him better, but I don't, because he might as well be dead. You see what I'm saying? My father's gone, he's history. So why be sad? And your mom is history, and that's the way it is." I spoke with my usual assurance. What a lie. Change the subject. "Garo, why do you like Fern Light?"

"Who?"

"Who, who, who? Are you an owl? Fern Light is a bigmouth. She's got something to say about everything. She's in my history class and she's always got her hand up."

"Her eyes . . ."

"They're bug eyes."

"Shut up." He leaped on top of me. "Take it back."

"Bug eyes." I threw him off and we banged around the room.

Mom thumped on the wall. "What are you boys doing?"

"Homework, Mom."

"When are you guys going to sleep, anyway?"

From the floor, Garo snored loudly.

"Very funny, Cal," Mom yelled.

"What if your father showed up here?" Garo asked. "What if he came right to this house and knocked on the door?"

I didn't know what to say, so I grunted. "Eaah."

"What if you didn't recognize him?"

"Eaah."

"Wouldn't it make you feel terrible?"

"He's never coming here."

"How do you know?"

"I know the way I know everything, Garo. I'm all knowing, all wise. Everything is revealed to me. I am in touch with cosmic secrets. Are you taking notes, Garo? Write it down in your jokebook."

# Chapter 5

"You coming?" I said. I bent down to check myself out in the mirror. I needed a haircut.

"Where you going?" Garo asked.

"Princesteins . . . then a haircut. You need one, too," I said. His curls were falling over his ears and into his eyes.

"I'm letting it grow down to my shoulders."

"Sixties look," I said. He didn't like having his hair cut. He always resisted.

"Boys," my mother yelled up the stairs. "Throw your clothes in the laundry."

"We did," I yelled back.

"Then change the sheets, and get that pigpen straightened up."

"Saturday warpath," I said. I looked around the room. It seemed okay to me. Garo picked up a pair of pants off the floor and hung them in the closet. He's neater than I am. He started to pull stuff out from under the bed.

"It's clean, it's clean," I said. "Let's go." Saturday mornings, once my mother gets done working us, we usually shoot baskets or hang around the playground to see if we can pick up a game. Today, though, I had a baby-sitting job.

"You're lucky," Garo said, on the way over to the Princesteins. "Most people won't ask boys to baby-sit their kids."

"I'm not lucky. Nobody wants to take care of their brats. I got the job by default."

"Did they really lock their mother in the cellar?"

"Could be," I said.

"They're good kids, just a little hyper." Garo likes kids, all kids, all types. He talks to them in the street. Why aren't people breaking down the door to get him to baby-sit? Because they look at Garo — his round face, his freckles — and he looks like one of their kids himself. And they think, Too young! Too young to be responsible. Then they look at me, and even though I'm younger than Garo, because I'm taller and look older, they think, Right. Ask him.

I do an okay job baby-sitting; I get by and the kids come out alive. But if I could get enough other work, I wouldn't baby-sit at all. I rake leaves in the fall, cut grass in the spring, shovel snow in the winter, and baby-sit if I have to.

"I'll be only two hours," Mrs. Princestein said

when we got there. "You think you can manage for two hours, Calvin? I just can't get back any sooner," she said apologetically.

"Sure, we'll be fine." She didn't even notice Garo.

"I'm flying, Mom!" Jamie screamed. Why do people think little girls are sweet and quiet? Jamie was jumping from the couch onto a chair, and then from the chair to the couch, and again from the couch to the chair. Every time she jumped, she screamed, "I'm flying, Mom!"

"Yes, darling. Uh, Cal — " Mrs. P. gestured vaguely at the living room. "Maybe you could get the kids to put some of their toys away?"

I looked around. The living room looked like a nuked toy store. The pillows were off the couch. The curtains were knotted. You couldn't take a step without crunching a red or blue toy. If the governor had been there, he would have declared it a disaster area and allocated funds for the victims.

"Nice place, Mrs. Princestein," Garo said politely.

"I'm flying, Mom!" Jamie screamed. "Watch me or I'll hit you!" She was little and blonde. Three years old. I think she was the one who locked her mother in the cellar.

Rick was walking around holding a toy telephone to his ear. "Come home now," he kept saying. "Come home now! Come home now." He was little and blond, also. Two years old, something like that.

"And, uh, Cal, if you could just wash up the

dishes while you're here," Mrs. Princestein said, getting her car keys. "Bye-bye, babies." She bent down to give Jamie and Rick kisses. "And wipe the cupboards, and give the floor a little sweep," she added.

She wanted me to take care of her little apes AND clean up her whole house? After she left, I got a good look at the kitchen. Another major disaster area.

". . . flying, Cal!" Jamie screamed, launching herself off the windowsill. Garo caught her, or she would have brained herself.

"Come home!" Rick threw his phone down. "Where's Mom?" He kicked me.

"Hey, it's not my fault she's gone."

He puffed out his lips, getting ready to cry.

"Hey," I said, "look, look!" I blew out my cheeks, then popped them with my fists, left, right. He liked that. He kept me popping my cheeks for five minutes. "Enough," I said. I was getting dizzy.

"More!" His lips puffed out again.

"Okay, okay, don't cry." I blew out my cheeks, popped them.

"I'm flying, Cal!" Jamie screamed. She was back on the couch.

"Come home now. Where's Mom?" Rick hiccupped.

"Do you think these kids are retarded?" I asked Garo. I sprawled on the couch and checked my watch. Ten minutes, and I was already going crazy.

"Never again," I said to Garo when we left.

"That was the longest two hours of my life."

"She pays good money, though."

"Yeah." I liked the feeling of the bills in my pocket. I wished my conscience didn't keep reminding me that half of it really belonged to Garo. He'd washed the dishes and played horsie with the two monsters. He'd probably worked harder than I had.

We stopped at Hair Today, where I always go to get my hair cut. So does Mom. It's one room, hair all over the floor, glossy posters on the wall, lots of mirrors and chairs, and two of those big pink plastic domes they put on ladies' heads when they're giving them permanents or something. Actually, I've seen guys under them, too.

"Hey, Cal," Fred said, when we walked in. "How you doing, baby?" He was cleaning the glass door that said UNISEX HAIR SALON. Fred works at Hair Today. Bob owns the place. "Sit down," Fred said. "You want a cut?" He was wearing a pink smock.

Bob waved to me. He was cutting an older woman's hair. They were talking about living in Buffalo and the terrible winters. "I couldn't wait to get out of there," Bob said, "and then I ended up here. You think the winters here are any better?"

Bob has a mustache and long straggly hair. He always looks like he needs a haircut himself. I think he's gay, but I'm not sure. I don't think Fred is, but I'm not sure about that, either. How can you really tell?

"So what's new with you guys?" Fred said.

He shampooed my hair, then I got in the chair and he started cutting. "You making waves with the girls, Cal?" He always says that; he was saying that when I was eight years old. I never answer.

But Garo! As if a button had been pressed, he started talking about girls, only not himself and girls. He had to talk about me and girls. He got into this whole Leslie Branch thing, telling Fred that she was hot for me.

"Shut up, Garo," I said.

"She told me so herself, Fred." Garo was sitting in the empty chair, twirling around. The higher he twirled the chair, the faster he talked. "You should see the valentines Calvin got. Leslie sent one with a red lipstick mouth."

"I'm not surprised," Fred said. "Look at that face on this kid." He pointed at me in the mirror.

"Yeah, Leslie says he looks like Clint Eastwood."

"Shut. Up," I muttered.

Fred winked at Garo. Then he called over to Bob. "You hear this, Bob? You see this face? We got a junior stud here."

I wanted to kill Garo and his big mouth.

Fred took off the sheet, dusted my collar, and handed me a mirror. He whipped the chair around so I could see the back of my head. "Okay," I said. I didn't even look.

"Just okay?"

What did he want, great? I jumped out of the chair and grabbed Garo. "Now do Garo, Fred."

"Hey!" Garo tried to squirm out of it. "I didn't

come for a haircut. I haven't got any money. I can't pay."

"Cut his hair, Fred. I'm paying." I threw all the money I'd earned down on the counter. Even if I didn't have enough for two haircuts, Bob would let me owe. "Cut, cut! He's going to look a lot better with a haircut."

Garo tried to get out of the chair, but I held him right there. "You don't have to shampoo him, Fred."

"What kind of a cut?" Fred asked, scissors raised.

Garo was still struggling. "I'm going to punch out your lights, Cal."

Just then, there was a tapping on the window. Three girls were looking in, smiling and waving. Three beaming faces, and we knew two of them — Fern Light and Angel Hayes. Superior and submissive, I said to myself. Snotty Fern, skinny Angel. The third girl was a black girl I didn't recognize. Extremely pretty.

"Hey, Garo," Fred said, "those girls are flirting with you, man." Garo straightened up, and Fred started cutting. Hair fell to the floor.

"What are you doing?" Garo said.

"Better behave, Garo," Fred said. "The girls have got their eyes on you."

I glanced over at the window. Angel Hayes was gone. But the black girl was bending over Fern's shoulder, and the two of them were watching.

Fred started by taking off just a little of Garo's hair. A little here, a little there. The curls were flying. When he got through, he held up the mirror for Garo. "How do you like it, Garo? I think it's really you."

Garo stared. Probably in shock. I was a little shocked myself. There was his hair all over the floor. There was his head sticking out nakedly. Fred had shaved Garo up the sides and back, leaving just a little lonely patch of curls on top.

# Chapter 6

When the phone rang, I licked peanut butter off my fingers and picked it up. "Hello."

"Cal, this is Alan."

"Hi, Alan." I knew it was him. I could always recognize his voice, rumbly and reassuring. Probably a perfect voice for an airline pilot: *Folks, we've got a little delay here, it seems the fuel gauge isn't working and one wing is drooping, while the emergency fiderator moderator is wacko, but not to worry, your captain will work out the bugs and we'll do like the birdies do.*

"I'm in Atlanta," Alan said.

"Want me to get Garo?"

"How are you doing, Calvin?" Alan asked.

"I'm okay, Alan." I had the phone between my ear and shoulder. I opened the refrigerator and looked around for what else to put on the sandwich.

"How's school going?"

"Okay," I said. "Good."

"You on the honor roll this time?"

"I think so."

There was a silence. I could almost hear Alan wondering what to say next. Our conversations were usually like this — both of us trying hard. "What'd you do this week, Captain A.?"

"Oh, good week. Good week. I've been having a really wonderful time! When you're with good people, good things happen. . . . Do you know what I mean?"

"Sure," I said. Sort of.

"Life can be inspiring when you're with the Perfect Person."

Here we go again, I thought. Alan's girlfriends were always Perfect Persons.

"And what'd you do that's exciting this week, Cal?" Captain Alan asked.

Hmm. Did he want to hear that I'd had a haircut on Saturday . . . aced a history test on Monday . . . and then been shot down by the coach today for being flat at basketball practice?

"Not too much, Alan. Ordinary week. Wait a minute, Alan." I yelled for Garo. He was upstairs. "Hold it, Alan. I'll get him."

I banged on the bathroom door. Garo was probably mournfully looking at his hair, or what had been his hair. I opened the door. I was right. "It looks good, Garo. It's already growing in."

"I'm not paying any attention to my bald head, Cal. I'm checking out my zits."

"You haven't got any zits. You've got a complexion like a baby's butt. Your father's on the phone. Move."

He picked up the phone upstairs in his father's room. I went downstairs and hung up. I poured milk and sat down to read the newspaper while I ate. I liked the letters from readers because people got so excited over such stupid things. *Dear Editor, Concerning Daniel Hawley's letter of the 16th about Kimberly Barnes letter of the 13th referring to your article on woolie bears of the 10th and the question why woolie bears cross the road, I have it on good authority . . .*

"Cal!" Garo called down. "My father wants you to say hello to Diane."

"Who?"

"Diane." Garo came to the top of the stairs. "Cal! Get the phone."

I pushed away from the table. "Hello?" I said.

"Hello!" the Perfect Person said. "You don't know me, but I feel like I know you." She had a little, almost squeaky voice. I wondered what she looked like. Maybe like Angel Hayes, who had the same sort of squeaky voice. "I've heard so much about you from Alan."

"Eaah . . ." My all-purpose grunt came in handy.

"I know you're like a second son to Alan."

"Eaah . . ."

"Can I call you Cal?"

"Sure."

48

"Cal, short for Calvin, right?"

"Right. Calvin Miller."

She laughed.

Was it funny? "You want to talk to Garo again?" I asked. And then I thought that if my father was ever inspired to call me, this would be exactly the way I'd feel — sort of overcome with muteness and slightly panicked.

Would this be the way my father would do it? Call me out of the blue and introduce a girlfriend? Did he even have a girlfriend? Maybe he'd taken a vow of celibacy. Or was he married again? I didn't know anything about him. He might even have another son. That thought made me feel really weird.

Later, when Garo and I were talking in our room, he said his father had been in a great mood because of Diane.

"Maybe he just likes Atlanta," I said.

Garo laughed his Eddie Murphy laugh. Heh. Heh. Heh. Heh. He was sitting on his bed, clipping his toenails.

"So what do you think, is Diane going to be for real? What's your opinion?" Garo asked me.

"My opinion is . . ."

A Garo toenail popped off, arced into the air, and landed on me.

". . . that your father always has more than one girlfriend."

Another toenail came boomeranging over. I scooped them up. "Keep 'em coming, Garo. I'm saving them for your cornflakes tomorrow morning. Add a little crunch. Did your father say anything?"

"He said the next time he goes down to Ft. Lauderdale, he's going to bring me back a lemon you can eat like an orange."

"Exciting."

"Yeah . . . so what do you think?"

"About lemons?"

"Get real. Did you hear anything that Diane said that made you think Dad's more, you know — serious this time? Does he mean business, do you think? When Dad and I were talking, I could hear her laughing in back."

"So what?"

"I don't know. She told me she's from this little mountain town in northern California. Redfield."

I lay back on the bed, my hands behind my head. "Well, there was something different, Garo. He's never asked me to talk to his perfect person before. That's new. And why would he tell her about me?"

"If he gets serious, he'll marry her."

"How do you know that?"

"He told me last time he was home that he's looking for the right person."

I whistled. "What would happen to Mom and me?" I asked, and then I answered myself. "We'd have to leave."

"Leave? You're not leaving! Don't be dense. Even if Dad got married, you wouldn't have to leave. Diane's got her own job. She's not going to stay home and wash dishes. She's a flight attendant."

"Excellent," I said, "your father's girlfriend is an airhead." I felt definitely relieved. This perfect person wouldn't last long. Alan was stuffy but too smart to marry someone dumb. Which led me to think about Angel Hayes and then Leslie Branch. Both of them would probably end up being airline flight attendants, too, or models, or something equally dumb.

"She's chairman of her union committee."

"Who?" I was still thinking about Angel and Leslie. Maybe I should kiss Leslie, since she was so interested, and at least find out what it was like.

"Diane," Garo said. "She's head of her union committee. I guess she can't be that much of an airhead, Cal."

I didn't know what to say to that, so I grunted. Grunts can be useful.

# Chapter 7

Friday night, our team, the Drumlins Hawks, had a home game against Martin Luther King Junior High. "You want me to come to the game tonight?" Mom said at supper.

"No. Why waste your time?"

"I don't mind, hon."

"Mom, we have a six-year unbroken record of losing to King. They're going to beat us; they always do. And I'm going to sit on the bench; I always do."

"You shouldn't be talking that way, Cal. You never know. Tonight could be your night to shine."

"Mom, in seventh grade, no matter how good you are, and I'm not that good, you always sit on the bench."

And that was the way things worked out. We lost and I sat on the bench. The two most memorable moments of the evening, for me, had nothing to do with the game, and both happened at halftime.

That's when I left the locker room and went out in the hall to get a drink of water. You weren't supposed to do that, you can get a drink in the locker room, but I just wanted to be by myself for a few minutes.

There was nobody in the hall. It was quiet and empty. Behind me I could hear the clatter from the locker room, and over my head, a muffled boom boom boom of a drum in the gym. Something moved at the end of the hall. I thought, *my father*. It was always at moments like this, when I was alone in an empty hallway or on a dark street that I thought of my father. And I'd somehow expect to see him coming around the corner. The feeling was so strong this time, I walked down to the end of the hallway.

That's when I saw two kids standing near an open locker, kissing. The boy was wearing glasses and a dark blue parka. The girl was wearing a red jacket. I bent over the fountain and water splashed up on my face. They were so engrossed in each other they didn't even notice me.

They kissed, then separated. The girl took two steps away, then reversed and went back to the boy, and they kissed again. They leaned toward each other and kissed, just their lips touching. Their lips held them together.

They separated again and then came back. They kept doing that, moving away from each other, then coming back and kissing, as if they couldn't bear to say good-bye.

My neck was hot. What would it be like to have a girl feel that way about me? The girl was so pretty, with long dark hair falling over the collar of her jacket.

I was mesmerized. I guess I would have stood there looking for as long as they stood there kissing, but Ralph Santano came out of the locker room and yelled, "Hey, Miller! You're wanted!" He had a towel around his neck. "Four more minutes," he called and went back into the locker room.

Just like that, the kissers disappeared.

I walked back toward the locker room. A girl dressed all in black came running down the stairs. "Cal!" It was Leslie Branch. Where had she come from? Maybe she really was a witch.

"Hi, Leslie." I wiped my mouth. I felt this . . . *something* . . . throbbing in my throat. I thought of the kissers. "What are you doing down here?" I asked.

She held up a lock. "You'll never guess what I did today. I locked my key in my locker. They had to smash my lock to get it open."

Did she still want to kiss me?

"You'd think they'd have a master key or something, wouldn't you?"

"Do you want to kiss me?" I blurted.

She tilted her head to the side and seemed to consider it. Her profile was like a cutout — those thin lips, her thin nose. Then she came up very close to me and said, "Okay."

*Okay?* Her face was right in front of my face. I felt a little crazy. Everything was banging and jarring in my body, like I had hearts pumping in my arms and legs and in the back of my head. I didn't know what to do. Put my arms around her? Everything seemed so complicated. Should I say something? Or did you just *do* it? Just kiss. What would happen to our noses? Would her nose spike me?

While I was thinking, Leslie was doing it. She kissed me. She put her mouth against mine, fitted her face to mine, and kissed me. She had the whole routine down perfectly. I say that with respect and admiration. It was wonderful. She took care of every problem.

Her lips didn't feel thin at all. It was amazing. She was amazing. It was nothing like the spin-the-bottle kisses I'd had at parties in grade school. I didn't want to stop. I forgot everything. My hands were sweaty, and I tried to hug Leslie.

She pulled away. "Don't you have to go back?" she said. "Sit on the bench some more?" She was smiling.

"Go back?" I asked dazedly. And then, over-head, I heard the whistle and the thud of guys running down the gym floor, and I realized the game had started again.

After the game, the coach called me into his office. "I'm sorry I was late," I said, as soon as I walked in.

"I don't think you're really interested in this team, Cal."

"I am."

"Well, I don't see it. You lack something."

"I'm sorry."

"That's not what I want. I don't like to hear that word on the team. Sorry is not good enough. I want you there. I mean your body, and I mean more than that. I want something from inside you, and if you don't have it, I can't give it to you."

"I'm sorry," I said again. How many times did that make? I wiped my hands down the sides of my shorts.

"What do you want to do with your life, Cal?" the coach asked.

I checked out my sneakers. What did my life have to do with this? I wanted to get my license when I was sixteen. That was all I knew about the future. Did I have to know more than that now? When I was still thirteen? Maybe if I had my father around, I'd know things. Sometimes I tried to talk to Mom about what I'd do when I got out of school, but she didn't have too many ideas for me. "Go to college," she always said. "Just go to college and then you'll figure it out from there. Honest to God, Cal, that's all I can tell you. I have enough trouble figuring out my own life."

The coach was waiting. "So have you got anything else to say for yourself?"

I shook my head. "Okay, go on, then." He waved his hand dismissingly. At least he didn't boot me off the team.

# Chapter 8

Alan held the back door of the car open for Mom. He was in civvies, but impressive-looking, anyway, in a pin-striped suit and vest. "I expect to hear some fine reports on you," he rumbled to Garo. He locked the car, and we all walked across the parking lot toward the lighted school entrance. Mom and I were behind Alan and Garo.

"Funny being driven around," Mom said. She was dressed entirely in red, except for her yellow pocketbook.

"Think we'll ever have a car?" I asked. Even though Mom used Alan's car all the time for shopping and stuff, it wasn't the same as having our own.

"Maybe when you get your license, we can buy a junker."

"I'm getting it when I'm sixteen," I said.

Ushers with sashes gave Mom and Alan a floor plan of the school as we entered. The school was mobbed. Lights were on everywhere, and there was a big banner across the wall in the front hall. WELCOME, PARENTS! Garo and I steered them toward the Language Arts lab, which we took the same period.

"So what do we do when we get there?" Alan said. "It's been a long time since I've been to one of these things."

"I know! It's a miracle that you're home on Parents' Night." Garo snapped the green striped suspenders Alan had brought him. "A real cool miracle."

"You have to sit in the seat and listen to the teacher," I said.

"Then stand in line to talk to the teacher," Garo said.

"I hope I don't fail this course," Alan said.

Mr. Pelter was in the doorway of the lab, holding his class record books under his arms. "Hello, Cal! Garo!" He held out his hand. He always reminded me of a stork. He was thin, with a large head, and stood sort of stooped over.

"This is my mother," I said. Mom gave me a jab in the back. "Mrs. Nina Miller," I added. Another jab, and I added, "And this is Mr. Pelter, Mom."

Mom's hand shot out. "So glad to meet you, Mr. Pelter," she said melodiously. "And this is Garo's father, Captain Alan Vitulli, Mr. Pelter."

I could see Mr. Pelter trying to work out who belonged to who, exactly. "You have, er, two very nice, er, sons," he said, looking somewhere between Mom and Alan.

What if Mom's friend Tom Lustig showed up? He was divorced and had a daughter in ninth grade, Sharon. What if Tom went up to Mom and put his arm around her? It would really confuse the situation.

"Alan goes with Garo," I blurted, "and Mom and I go together." Then I felt stupid.

But Mr. Pelter looked relieved and said, "Cal could be one of my star pupils, Mrs. Miller. Except he doesn't try hard enough. He doesn't push himself. He gets good marks, but he could be so much better."

More parents appeared, and Mr. Pelter transferred his attentions to them. Mom and Alan went into the classroom, and Garo and I went out in the corridor to wait for them.

"Star Pupil," Garo said.

"I don't know where he gets that stuff."

"You're good at writing."

I shrugged. "I'm okay."

"I could see Dad hoping Pelter would boast about me, too."

"He didn't boast, Garo. He complained."

"I might fail history this section."

"History? You're going to fail history? That easy class?"

"I hate dates."

"So don't eat them."

Garo stepped on my foot. "Leave the jokes to me."

"Is Alan going to be mad about you failing? I could help you out, if you want me to."

"I didn't say I was definitely going to fail. I said I might. Mr. Aketa said, 'You have a choice, Garo. You can work or you can goof off . . .'" He got Aketa's voice down pretty good. Then he gave his laugh. Heh! Heh! Heh! Heh!

The door of the lab opened. Parents streamed out. Mrs. Jones-Barbarra, the Second Vice-Principal, was walking down the hall, greeting people and shaking hands with parents. Mrs. J-B is fairly beautiful for an older person. She was wearing a gold and white striped dress and her eyes were made up with greenish gold stuff on the eyelids. She's about as different from the First Vice-Principal as peaches are from poison. The First V-P is Mr. Stark, a total hair shirt. He does all the discipline stuff. He never shows up at functions like this, just when something unpleasant is happening.

Mrs. Jones-Barbarra stopped as Mom and Alan came out of the lab, and I did the introductions again. "Calvin Miller's mother," Mrs. Jones-Barbarra said. "How nice to meet you." She looked like a model next to Mom.

"Calvin's ma," Mom said. "You can always tell me. I'm short and fat, and I carry a yellow purse."

Why did she have to say that about herself? It was corny. It was a put-down. I walked away.

"Where're you going, hon?" Mom called. They must have heard her all over the building.

"I saw Fern Light," Garo said. He was trying to sound casual, but he was excited and grinning. "I saw her with her parents." Then he seemed to realize he was talking a lot about Fern. "I saw a lot of kids," he said sort of lamely.

Garo and I were in the gym with Mom and Alan, our last stop, when Leslie Branch tapped Garo on the shoulder. "Hi, Curly," she said.

She didn't even speak to me. Didn't she remember the kiss? I'd been thinking about it a lot. If I concentrated, I could almost make it happen again in my mind.

"Garo, did I tell you I lo-o-o-ve that haircut," she said. "Very cool." She winked at Garo and went off.

The drill team came out on the floor, and we stood around and watched. I was sorry right away, because the coach was right there, in his white shorts and white T-shirt, his arms crossed over his chest. He checked out our whole group, then his light blue eyes landed on me.

"Isn't that your coach?" Mom said. "You should introduce us."

"Mom, he's busy." I sort of steered her toward the seats. Every time the coach looked our way, I slid down on my spine. I should have looked him straight in the eye, held up my head, the sort of thing you read about people doing in books. I knew he was right about me. I didn't have enough drive and purpose. I liked the idea of being on the team, but I didn't go out for it with my whole heart like some guys did. It was a depressing thought.

On the way out of school, I had another depressing thought — that I was just another notch on Leslie Branch's belt. Just one more kiss on her way to the *Guinness Book of World Records*.

# Chapter 9

Garo and I were in the mall downtown in the city, shopping. Garo likes to shop. I pretty much hate it. The plan was, shop first, then hit the library. We could have split up, me to the books, him to the stores, but we like keeping each other company.

We didn't get straight down to business. We went into the record shop first and browsed. Then we got hungry and bought slices of pizza. Then to the department store and the underwear department. I started yawning right away.

"What's your problem?" Garo said.

"Bored." I don't mind being given new things, but the work of finding them bores me silly.

Garo was right at home picking up socks and color matching them against the undershorts. "Look at this, Cal, an almost perfect match."

"Why do your socks and shorts have to match?"

"It's style, Cal. Style matters!"

"Are you telling me what you wear on your butt is a matter of importance?"

"To me, yes. Now here, look at these." He held up a pair of shorts. "Close, but not the color blue I want. I want something with more bounce."

"If I need socks — " I said.

"I know, I know, you just go out and buy socks."

"Right. And if I need shorts, as long as they fit — "

"You're satisfied," he finished for me. "Do you like these green ones? Look at this!" He held up a pair with hearts on them. "Now if I could find a pair of socks with red hearts — "

We must have spent an hour before Garo got what he wanted. Half a dozen pairs of color-coordinated shorts and socks. Garo looked happy. A satisfied shopper.

"On to the library," I said.

"Sure, sure." Now it was Garo's turn to yawn. Just the thought of a roomful of books could do that to him.

We were almost to the cashier when Garo said in an odd voice, "Cal . . . look!" His freckles had lit up like neon signs.

"What?" I didn't see anything out of the ordinary, just shoppers and a few suspicious-looking people who were probably store detectives.

"Cal . . . is that Fern Light working at the checkout?"

I looked at the dark-haired girl. "Could be. Did you know she worked here?"

"No! What do I do now? I can't check out *there*," he said in an agonized voice.

"Why not? She doesn't care what color your socks are."

"Cal! Underwear!"

"Fern's a big girl, Garo. She knows you wear underpants."

He stood frozen, clutching his packages and staring at Fern and mumbling about what she'd say.

"She's the girl you like, isn't she?" I asked.

"No," he said.

"Why don't you just admit it?"

"She's not the one. It's just, it's just . . ."

"It's just that you think I've got brain damage, boy. Fern is the one."

"Okay, okay, but I don't want to hear you telling me you don't like her, Cal."

"I don't. So kill me."

"I don't want to hear that from you, Cal! Not from my best friend!" He tried to hit me. He must have forgotten he had all those packages. They went flying. Plastic-wrapped shorts and socks on little plastic hangers all over the floor.

"Fern's the one." I piled stuff in his arms. "I knew it! Why *her*?"

"Why don't you like her? She's a terrific girl, she's smart, she's beautiful, and she's — "

" — got a big sarcastic mouth," I finished for him.

He peered toward the checkout counter. Fern was half hidden by a display of scarves. "You don't really know her. She's not sarcastic, she's slightly, uh, slightly — "

"Slightly superior," I suggested.

"Ease up," Garo begged. "You don't know what it feels like to feel this way."

"I know what it feels like to kiss a girl," I said suddenly.

He turned toward me. "Who?"

"Leslie."

"You kissed Leslie?"

"Yes."

"Cal! You didn't tell me." He looked over toward Fern again. "Are you sure that's her? I can't check this stuff out with her."

"Oh, sure you can. What's the big deal?" There I was, with my confident-sounding voice. Man of the world. As if I'd checked out dozens of pairs of underwear with dozens of girls. "Look," I said, "just go up there, put down your stuff. Act casual, make some conversation, take out the money. Pay. She'll see what a nice guy you are."

"Don't you think she knows I'm a nice guy?"

"She may think you're a fool. You tell too many jokes around her. Be cooler. Don't say so much."

"Shh! She'll hear you." We walked the long way around and approached the counter from the other side. By the time we got there, Fern had left the checkout and was heading for the escalator. We followed her up to the third floor, to the package wrapping counter. When we got there, we saw it wasn't Fern. It was someone else, who, when we got up close, hardly looked like Fern at all.

After Garo paid for his stuff, we headed for Ben and Jerry's for ice cream, to revive us, as Garo said. "I sort of knew it wasn't Fern," Garo said. "I guess I was just hoping."

"Would you have talked to her?" I said, and then I saw my father.

I saw him coming out of the bank next to Penny's. I saw a tall man in a sport jacket. A tall man, slightly balding, in a worn blue sport jacket.

I walked toward him. Garo was saying something. I kept walking toward the man in the blue jacket. Garo called me, I think. My father was moving toward the exit. I walked faster, keeping his tall, slightly stooped figure in sight.

Then he was at the revolving door to the parking lot, and I ran. He was in the door. I pushed past people, through the door, into the parking lot. He was gone.

# Chapter 10

I didn't tell anyone about "seeing" my father. It must have been a mirage, seeing what I wanted to see — like Garo's mirage of "seeing" Fern. What had Garo said? *I guess I was just hoping.* That would fit me, too, I suppose, although there was a difference. I didn't even know I was thinking about my father, whereas Garo was definitely aware that he was thinking about Fern.

Did I say thinking? Talking would be more accurate. Now that her name was out in the open, I couldn't shut him up about her. He woke up in the morning with her name coming out of his mouth. He talked through breakfast and then all the way to school. It was how he'd seen Fern in the music room . . . and Fern's eyes . . . and did I know Fern was running for Student Senate? But in school, if he saw her, not a word. He went mum, silent, mute. He just blushed and walked by her.

"Garo, you're all talk and no action," I said. We were in our room.

Garo rubbed his head, dug his fingers into his scalp where he'd been shaved. The hair was starting to come back, and it was itching him like crazy. "I know. What should I do? I can't say anything to her. She'll laugh at me," he said. That was one breath. The next was, "Should I call her, Cal? Maybe I could talk to her if it was on the phone."

"Good idea."

"It is? . . . No, I don't know her number."

"I'm sure Mom will let you borrow the phone book, Garo."

"What would I say?"

"You could start with hello."

"Hello," he practiced. "Hello, Fern."

"Put a little more punch into it, Garo."

"Hello, Fern! . . . How's that?"

"Great. You'll blow out her eardrums."

"Hello?" He paused. "Fe-e-e-rn?" He looked at me.

"Can you do it without sounding like you're not sure that's her name?"

"Hello? Is this Fern?" He stood in front of the mirror. "Hello. . . . This is Fern, isn't it?" He put his hand to his ear, as if he were holding a phone. "Hello! Fern Light? . . . Hello. Fern Light, Garo here! . . . I'll never get it right. You do it, Cal. Call her for me."

"And what am I supposed to say? Fern, this

70

is Calvin Miller, and I'm calling for my shy friend Garo. . . . He's not too bright but he's got a good heart."

"I'm not shy. I'm just having a little trouble with this now."

"I know and I don't understand it. Why all this trouble about making a phone call?"

"Cal, don't you understand anything? This isn't just calling any girl. And even if I do it, what am I going to talk about?"

"Buying candy-striped underpants," I suggested.

He threw a pillow at me. "Get serious." The phone rang, and he froze. "What if it's *her?*"

"It would be another miracle," I said. "A superior cool miracle." I went across the hall to Alan's bedroom. It couldn't be Fern. Too much of a coincidence. Or my father . . . But when I picked up the phone and heard a man's voice, for a moment I thought . . . No, I don't know what I thought. I stopped thinking.

"Cal? This is Tom Lustig."

It took me another moment to get myself together again. Then I said, "You want Mom, Tom?"

"No, you, Cal. How would you like to model for me? You and Garo. I need two wholesome-looking kids for this assignment. If you can do it, I want you at the studio next week. I'll pay you regular rates," he added.

"Okay," I said.

"Okay, you'll do it? Don't you want to talk to Garo?"

"No, he'll do it. We'll be there."

"You know where the studio is, don't you?" Tom asked.

"Sure." I'd gone there with Mom the time she did the Wate Pow(d)er session.

"You take the bus into the city — "

"Right, I know."

"It's the Number Five," Tom said, "and you can pick it up — "

"I can get there okay, Tom."

Mom went by in the hall and stopped. "Who's that?" she said.

"Tom," I said. "He wants me and Garo to model."

Tom was still giving me directions. He has a tendency to overinstruct. I held the phone away from my ear and made the bla bla bla sign with my hand to Mom.

"Tom, this is Nina," she yelled. "Stop treating my son like an idiot."

I handed her the phone and went back to Garo. "Hey, Garo, we're going to be models."

I knew he wouldn't mind. But not only didn't he mind, he went a little loony with excitement. "I'm a model," he lisped, and he started mincing around, swinging his hips. He put a sock on his head like a hat and tied a shirt around his waist. "I'm going to be a famous, beautiful model. Where's my lipstick? Where's my eye mascara, or whatever you call that stuff."

"Now you have something you can talk about to Fern," I said.

"Tell her I'm going to be a model?" He staggered. "You're crazy. You ever hear of a boy being a model?"

"Are you serious? Open a magazine. Guys are models all the time."

"Gay ones," he said.

"Don't be so stupid." I suddenly tipped up his bed and buried him under his blankets and stuff. When he started to crawl out, I sat on him.

Mom pounded on the wall. "Stop making so much noise, I'm on the phone."

"We'll be quiet," I shouted, just as Garo got his arm around my neck and sent me crashing.

# Chapter 11

Saturday morning, while we were eating breakfast, we listened to Bud Droger on the radio reviewing a new movie, *Crazy Raisins*. "Shut him off," Garo said. He didn't like Bud Droger.

"I want to hear him." I like movies, and I like reading and hearing reviews about them. I like Droger, too, even though the last time he drooled over a movie — he called it something like "an instant classic of perverse humor" — I privately thought it was totally asinine.

"If I did movie reviews," Garo said, "they'd be short and sweet. I'd say, '*Fast Guns* is a bunch of crap!' Or, 'I give *Avery Avery* ten stars!' Or, 'Run, don't walk to see *Tickle Me Quick!*' I'd be right to the point. Not like windy Droger."

Droger gave *Crazy Raisins* five thumbs-up. "A belly whopper," he said. "A hilarious fresh surprise, an original fantasy with a totally amazing twist at the end."

"So let's go," I said. "It sounds great." Then I remembered I didn't have any money.

"I'll treat," Garo said.

"No, you won't."

"I'll make you a loan, then."

"No."

"Cal, don't be so stiff-necked. You're going to work tomorrow morning for Mrs. Princestein, and next week you'll make more money from Tom."

"Okay, but I pay you back right away."

We wanted to go to the early showing, but Mom had other ideas. The weather had warmed up and Mom said it was time for our first outdoor spring cleaning. "Get the rakes, Cal. Garo, get the plastic bags. Hop to it, boys." She kept us busy right up to movie time.

Walking to the theater, I started thinking about Garo as a talk show host. When he was famous, people would quote his opinions on movies, too. And on food and records and books. That would be really cool. I could see him in the studio, sitting in front of the mike with earphones on, zinging in a cassette for a song, then taking a call, listening and answering, making someone feel good. I knew just what his life was going to be. I probably thought more about Garo's future than mine. Mine was just a big dark blank to me.

There was a line of kids waiting to buy tickets. They'd probably all heard Bud Droger that morning. We got in line, and there was Fern and Angel Hayes in front of us. Talk about timing! If we'd spent five more minutes raking the yard . . . or come for the first show, we'd have missed them.

When Garo saw the girls, it was just like when he heard that Tom wanted us to model. He went loony. He started talking in a loud, excited voice about — you're not going to believe this — cockroaches.

"Did you hear about the new breed of cockroaches? They look like regular cockroaches, but they fly, and they like light instead of dark. You know what that means? They're right there in the house with you like your cat or your dog. They crawl up the walls, they get on your TV, they swarm up the table, they get in the food."

Fern and Angel turned around. "Do I hear a familiar voice?" Fern said in her usual sarcastic manner. Her eyebrows started wagging like flags in a high wind.

Garo's mouth was going even faster than her eyebrows. "I heard that down in Florida, if you go outside on the lawn, you step into squashy piles of them. They crawl up your legs, they fly into your hair, they creep into your ears and your nose. Can you imagine a cockroach in your nose?"

"Uggg!" Angel shuddered.

"Hi, Garo," Fern said. "I guess you must like cockroaches. You sound so enthusiastic about them."

"Yeah," Garo said lamely. He seemed to have

run out of breath and talk at the same moment. "They're, uh, interesting," he said. I guess he couldn't believe he was actually talking to her.

"I read about those roaches," Fern said. "They're moving up north. This way, actually. In about a year, some people think they might make it all the way up here." She glanced at me. "Then they'll be living in *our* cities and getting in *our* houses."

"And ears and noses," I said, under my breath.

"Excuse me?" Fern said, ultrapolitely.

"Forget it."

"Excuse me?" she said again. "Did you say something? Did you make a contribution to this conversation?"

What a witch. I didn't bother answering her. I stared across the street, as if I saw something of great interest out there. And I did. Because the same spooky thing happened again that had happened last week in the mall. I "saw" my father. Or, anyway, I saw that same tall, skinny man wearing dark pants and a blue sport jacket.

I knew it couldn't be my father. He wasn't here. He was in Maine.

No, I didn't actually know that. That was only where he'd sent the last postcard from. Three years ago. Right now he could be in Mexico or Mozambique or Massachusetts. Or Moravia. Or Outer Mongolia. He could be anywhere in the world, so why would he be here?

Anyway, it wasn't him. He had more hair than that man. And he was taller. And why would he still be wearing the same blue sport jacket he'd worn nine years ago?

I crossed my arms, clasped my hands onto my elbows and held on, held myself back from running across the street. Held onto myself and told myself all this sensible stuff, all these good sensible reasons why that man going out of sight could not be my father.

The line was moving forward. "Come on, Cal!" Garo beckoned me, holding up the tickets.

In the lobby, I stopped to buy popcorn. "I'll get the seats," Garo said.

When I went into the theater, I looked toward the back row, where we usually liked to sit. But then I saw Garo, down in the middle, sitting right behind Angel and Fern.

When I sat down he dug into the popcorn, a big handful, dropping half of it. I thought he was going to pass out with excitement. Or choke himself the way he was stuffing his mouth, then gulping it all down. Suddenly he leaned forward between the two girls. "You want some popcorn?"

"I'll have a little," Fern said. She gave me a sarcastic glance. "If it's okay with your silent friend."

"Don't get it stuck in your teeth," I muttered.

The girl had hearing like a bat. "Oh, thank you for the advice. So glad you told me, Calvin! I left my *How to Eat Popcorn Guide Book* at home today!"

I slumped down in the seat, then sat up straight, aware that Fern was watching me from the corner of her eye. Then slumped again. What did I care if she was watching me? I tried to ignore her. She was talking and laughing with Angel. I caught a word here, a word there.

The lights went out, the movie came on. I watched the giant figures on the screen. People were moving around rapidly, laughing and gesturing. Afterward, I could hardly remember the movie. What I did remember was that man. That skinny man in the worn blue jacket.

# Chapter 12

"A blue sport jacket, Mom," I said. I was telling her about the man I'd seen in the mall and then again across the street from the movies.

"Uh-huh. You know what we have to do now, Cal? I just read that we should soak the veggies in detergent." She was at the sink. "Detergent! That makes you feel good about what you're eating."

Didn't she hear me? "Mom, I saw this same guy two times. He looked just like that picture of my father. That's pretty weird, isn't it?"

"You're supposed to soak them for twenty-five minutes to get off all the pesticides."

"Mom, are you listening?"

"I hear you," she said. "Same guy, blue jacket, weird coincidence. Right?"

"Right." I couldn't figure out the smile on her

face. Half smile. Automatic smile. Not a real smile. Maybe she thought I wanted to talk about my father, which was never a favorite thing with her. I didn't want to do that. Or did I? I felt mad that she was talking about vegetables.

"Why'd you and my father get married if you were just going to split up six years later?" I said.

"Who knew that was going to happen, Cal? I was feeling lonely. My mother had died, and your father — well, he was there."

"He was *there?* You mean anybody would have done?"

"I didn't say that. You make it sound like — what do you want to know, Cal?"

"Did you like him?"

"He was a nice enough man, but he didn't know how to stick to things."

"What things?"

"Anything. That's why he was a salesman, not because he was such a great personality, but just because he could always leave one job and get another."

"What kind of things did he like?"

Mom frowned. "How do I know, Cal? It's a long time ago. It's behind me. I don't want to talk about this anymore."

So I shut up. But what I thought was, Maybe it's behind you, but it isn't behind me. I didn't even know what I meant by that.

Mr. Aketa was late coming into history class, and everyone was fooling around. Kids were sitting on their desks, talking across the room to each other. A boy everyone called Grandpa because of his glasses sat down behind Mr. Aketa's desk and put up his feet. "Attention, class! Attention!"

The rules of the room were posted on the wall. PLEASE MAINTAIN QUIET. STAY IN YOUR SEATS. NO INAPPROPRIATE LANGUAGE. NO TALKING WHEN SOMEONE ELSE IS TALKING. At that moment, every single rule was being broken.

"Maybe they're giving birth," Fern said, over the racket. "It'll be a notable moment in history."

Mr. Aketa's wife was pregnant, but when he'd told us about it, he said, *"We're* going to have a baby." He kept us informed. "You kids'll be the first to know when it happens." He liked to talk about being pregnant. "We had a sonogram," he told us. "We think we're going to have a boy." He had us all suggest names and picked Kenneth Mason. Garo was the one who suggested Kenneth, which was for Mr. Aketa's father. Mason was Mrs. Aketa's family name.

Leslie Branch wrote the date on the board. That was the first thing Mr. Aketa always did. He was very organized. Leslie wrote the way she looked — thin, energetic letters. "Anybody want me to write anything else?"

"Your score," Evan Fisher called from the back of the room where he always sat.

Leslie smiled calmly, her thin nose quivered. I wondered if she'd already kissed Evan. She put down the chalk and went back to her seat. A moment later I heard her saying to Fern, "I feel out in the cold; he really rejected me."

Who? Evan? That oaf? Or was she looking at me? I shifted nervously in the seat. Did she think I rejected her? Had she wanted me to ask for another kiss? I'd been willing! She'd been the one who told me to go back into the gym. I reminded myself of her Guinness Record ambitions. She could be talking about any one of fifty boys rejecting her.

I opened a book and started reading. A not very good science fiction novel. Over the top of the book, I watched Leslie and Fern. Fern was talking. She waved her arms around emphatically. What would it be like to kiss her? How could you even manage it? You'd miss the target. She'd never shut up for a second.

Suddenly Leslie and Fern both turned and looked at me. I raised my book and sank down in my seat. Why did I sink down like that? They'd think I was hiding from them . . . but if I straightened up now, they'd think I did *that* for them, too. I stared at the page. "Thirppy Zee, turn the Mun Scrolls. Hurry! Lock it up!" I read the same sentences over and over.

What if I got up and ambled over to the girls? Just did it, straight-backed and cool. Sat down near them, put my feet up on a desk, crossed my arms over my chest, and said, *So what's new and interesting with you two ladies?*

Leslie would flash her eyes and quiver her nose. I'd give her a meaningful look. Fern's eyebrows would start wagging, and she'd make one of her sarcastic remarks. *Leslie! Lucky us! Calvin wants to know what's new! Oh, thank you, Calvin. I was having a crisis of boredom!*

I'd ignore Fern; I'd be extremely composed. I'd tell them about the book I was reading, *Thirppy Zee and the Sercovian Prophecy.* Science fiction is usually excellent, I'd say. Lots of interesting ideas. But this one, yu-u-u-ck. I'd toss it aside. *Oh, what a stimulating book review,* Fern would say. *You have such an inspiring way with words, Calvin.*

Okay, scratch that. I'd tell them about Garo and me modeling for Tom. That would do it. They'd go crazy. Girls were always impressed by models. I'd say, *Did you ever try and look happy for two hours straight?*

Tom's job was to do a photo for a boxed set of birthday stuff: tablecloth, napkins, favors, party hats, etc. It was aimed at kids younger than us, but Tom said the manufacturer had done market research. "Which proved," he said, "that a picture of older kids on the package, especially boys, especially good-looking guys like you two, sold the product best."

Garo and I had to hang out in front of a decorated table covered with the birthday stuff and a huge frosted birthday cake. "Look handsome, guys," Tom said. "Look happy."

I thought modeling would be a cinch. Take a picture, collect your money, and go. Forget it. Something was wrong with every shot. Either the lighting was too strong or too weak, or the tablecloth didn't show up properly, or Garo moved, or I didn't look happy enough. It took

Tom two hours and three rolls of Polaroid film before he was satisfied and ready to take THE picture, the final picture, for the manufacturer. The one that would go on the box.

I sneaked another look at Leslie and Fern over the top of the book. Would they want to hear all that? Was it interesting or boring?

Suddenly, Mr. Aketa came running into the room. "It's time, kids," he cried.

"For what?" Raymond Rogers asked.

"For the baby, stupid," Grandpa said. He leaped out of Mr. Aketa's chair.

Mr. Aketa started stuffing things into his briefcase. "Good-bye, kids."

"Good-bye, Dad," Leslie called.

Mr. Aketa walked out, then came running back in. "Kids! Did I say it? We're having a baby. Kids, don't let me down." His face was red, and he was smiling all over the place.

And that's when it came to me why Mom's smile yesterday had seemed so strange. That smile when I was telling her about the man in the blue jacket. Because Mom always looked you full in the face when she talked to you, thrust her face right at you, and when she smiled it was five hundred watts. Like Mr. Aketa's smile right now. But yesterday, her eyes had been down and *shut*. That was what had made her smile so different, so un-Momish. It had been a smile of closed eyes — as if she didn't even want to see me.

"Kids, Mrs. Jones-Barbarra is coming to look in on you, soon," Mr. Aketa said. "Study your books, okay? Don't riot. I'll see you tomorrow."

I wondered if my father was that excited when I was born. Did he think it was neat that he was having a baby? A son? Did he go to the hospital with Mom? Did he run around telling people? Did he say, *We're having a baby!* Did he smile like he'd just won a million bucks?

# Chapter 13

"What's the occasion?" I asked.

"Can't I take you and Garo out to breakfast on a Sunday morning without a reason?" Mom gunned the engine at a red light.

"You never did before."

"Oh, come on, sure I did." She snapped her fingers. "Last year, we went out to breakfast at the hotel. You forgot that, huh?"

"Brunch," Garo said. "It was brunch, Nina. It was great. I never saw so much food in one place. They had sausages that were the best I ever tasted."

"That was for your birthday, Mom," I said. "What is this for?"

"What a suspicious boy." Mom pulled the car into the parking lot. "Maybe it's my birthday again."

We walked across the gravel lot toward a small pink stone building. The restaurant was called Le Bread and Buttery. Mom held the door open. "Be nice, Cal," she said, as we walked in.

What did that mean? What did I do wrong? Ask a question?

Le Bread and Buttery was a long narrow room. Plants hung from the ceiling. In front was an old-fashioned glass display case with food set out like prizes or presents on the shelves. On top there was a big wheel of dark yellow cheese and a long loaf of French bread with a knife next to it. In the case under it was a row of pies with fluted edges. A small white card said QUICHE LORRAINE. Another card said BLUE CHEESE PIE.

"I'll have one of each," Garo said.

We sat down at a wooden table. A boy sitting on a bench in the window was writing away, his head bent in concentration. He had a note-book on his lap, other books spread open around him.

"He's a college student," Mom said. "Look at the way he's studying, hon. Bet he gets good marks."

"Look at the way Garo's studying," I said. He had his nose right in the menu.

"Can I get anything I want, Nina?" he asked.

"Within reason."

"That means don't break the bank," I said.

Mom looked in her purse. "I have thirteen, no, almost fourteen dollars. You guys go ahead and have a good time. I'm just going to have a slice of bread and a cup of coffee."

Garo decided to have sausages and French waffles with whipped cream. I ordered bacon and buckwheat pancakes with strawberry sauce. "French bread and coffee," Mom said to the waitress.

"French bread — is that on the menu?" the waitress asked. She had dark tired eyes.

"No, no, but it's right there." Mom stood up and pointed to the loaf of French bread. Why did she have to stand? She had her yellow pocketbook over her shoulder, and it slipped and fell to the floor. Some people at other tables turned and looked at us.

"That's probably not even real bread, Nina," Garo said.

"Oh, yes, it's real," the waitress said.

"Then I want a slice," Mom said. She put her purse next to her. "With coffee."

"We don't cut that loaf." The waitress had her pencil poised over the pad. "Anything besides the coffee?"

"Why don't you cut the bread? If it's to attract your customers, it would look much better sliced," Mom argued. "More appetizing. I expect you to charge me for it. But not too much," she added.

"Mom, it's not on the menu," I said, pinching her arm. "Let it go."

She jerked away. "Cut that out, Cal."

The waitress flipped her pad and left.

"Do you always have to say something about everything?" I said to Mom. "Why can't you do things regular?"

"Garo," she said, leaning across me, "did I ever tell you about when I was in high school and taking Driver Education?"

"I didn't know they had Driver Ed in those days," Garo said.

"You mean back in them olden days? Way back then? Why, as a matter of fact, we didn't, Garo honey. What we had was Dinosaur Ed, the finer points of how to harness and ride a dinosaur."

"Heh heh heh heh," Garo heh-hed.

"Heh heh heh heh," Mom heh-hed back.

I felt like killing them both.

"So, anyway," Mom said, still leaning across me, "there I am, Garo, doing great, star pupil and all that. I've got this whole driving thing checked out. And then it's time for me to take the test. The big day."

She shot a tiny glance at me to see if I was listening. I had my hands behind my head, my legs stuck out sideways in the aisle. The tables were about big enough for two kindergarten kids.

"So the other kids are telling me, 'Nina, watch out for so and so,' who's the tester. I think his name was Lester. Lester the tester. He was a mean dog; the other kids said he'd look for any reason to flunk you. So I tell myself, Not me. Not little Nina. I'm going to do everything right with Lester the tester, and to begin with I'm directly on time. I'm there before him, I'm waiting, all eager and fresh. The moment he gets in the car, I'm looking for points. I say, 'Would you

90

like to buckle up your seat belt, sir?' I'm letting him know I remember everything. Star pupil. He gives me one sour look and says, 'NO, I WOULDN'T LIKE TO BUCKLE UP MY SEAT BELT. I WANT TO BE ABLE TO JUMP OUT AND SAVE MY LIFE!' "

"Heh! Heh! Heh! Heh! Great story, Nina," Garo said.

"Like it, Cal?" Mom said. "Funny?"

"Not bad," I admitted.

"You ever heard that before, hon?"

"No, Mom."

"I should tell you more stories about me."

The waitress brought the food. We started eating. "I sure wish I had that piece of French bread to go with the coffee," Mom said. She elbowed me. "Got mad at your ma, didn't you?"

"I wasn't mad."

"No, I guess that wasn't steam I saw coming out of your ears." She forked a piece of pancake off my plate and tasted it. "I make better," she said.

We were just about done eating when Mom said, "There is actually another story I should tell you, Cal. Sort of an up-to-date story. The reason we're here this morning."

"I knew there was something you were holding back."

"Okay, don't be so smart."

I shrugged. I felt as if my ears were twitching like a rabbit's. Maybe I knew before she said it what she was going to say.

"I suppose you're going to get mad at me for

this, hon, but I had my reasons." Mom fiddled with her purse, opening and closing the metal clasp. "You probably did see your father."

I put down my knife and fork. I felt as if someone had just punched me in the stomach. So I *had* seen him! "Wipe your mouth," I said to Garo. He had syrup all over it. I shoved his napkin at him.

"He showed up about a week ago," Mom said softly — what was softly for her, probably just normal voice for anyone else.

"How come you didn't tell me?"

"I'm telling you now."

"He was at the house, he came right there?"

Mom nodded. Next to me, Garo had stopped eating.

"A week ago?" I said. "Why did you wait all this time to tell me?" I imagined my father at the door, pressing the bell, listening, maybe brushing down the sleeves of the old blue sport jacket.

Mom's face was flushed. "I don't know, Cal. I just kept putting off telling you . . . and then, somehow . . . I thought it would be easier to tell you here. I mean, a nice place . . . it would make it easier to tell you."

I felt like saying, *And did it?* I felt stupid and hot. "What did he say?" I asked.

Mom shrugged. "Not too much. He, uh, wanted to see you." She kept opening and closing the clasp on her pocketbook. "He said — well, that's what he said. That he came to see you." She looked up, half smiling. "I knew he didn't come to see me!"

"And what'd you say?"

"I said hello. And then, if you want to know, I told him he had a damn nerve, and I sent him away."

"Why?" Garo asked, leaning over me.

"Shut up, Garo," I said. "Just shut up." But then the waitress came over with our bill, and we all shut up. We didn't say anything again until we were outside.

"So, are you mad at your mom?" Mom said as we walked across the parking lot.

"No."

"Yes, you are."

"No, I'm not!"

"Well, you can be mad at me, Cal. I don't blame you, in a way. I just want you to understand — "

"Why'd you tell him he had a nerve?" I interrupted. "Why'd you say that?"

"You don't think I should have said it? He doesn't know you're alive for nine years, and then he shows up and says he wants to see you? Just like that! Like it's his due? Like it's coming to him. What did he ever do for you?" she asked. "Tell me that."

Her voice got louder and louder. I'm so stupid I was just thinking how glad I was that we'd left the restaurant. But I couldn't get away from her words.

"I'm the one who raised you, Cal, who supported you, who worried about us and got us set. That man didn't ever do one damn thing for you, Cal." She was breathing hard. "And if you want to know the whole story, he borrowed forty dollars from me. How about that! I gave him forty dollars. Am I a fool or aren't I?"

"Why did you do it?"

She lifted her shoulders and grimaced. "Why? I don't know why. Because I'm a sucker. Because he knows how to ask for those things and make you feel guilty if you don't give them to him."

"But you didn't feel guilty telling him he couldn't see me." I tried to keep my voice neutral. I felt confused. Mad at my mother, but at the same time feeling wrong about it, thinking I shouldn't feel that way. She was right, wasn't she? My father had never shown any interest. What was I supposed to do, fall down in awe because he got a whim to see me now?

"Listen, Cal, don't hard-time me," she said.

"I'm not hard-timing you, Mom. I didn't say anything."

"Maybe you think I should have invited him in? Well, I didn't. He showed up, I gave him forty bucks and sent him away. Now he'll stay away for another eight years."

"Okay, fine with me," I said. "Let's forget it."

But as if I'd protested, she went right on. "Well, what was I supposed to do? Give him tea and crumpets? Pat him on the back for being Father of the Year? Tell him he's a great guy for finally wanting to see his own son? Or did he want that? Now that's a question, isn't it, Cal?

94

How much did he want to see you, how much did he want to get forty bucks from me?"

My face flashed hot. "Let it go," I said. "Just let it go!"

We got in the car. Mom put the key in the ignition. "Okay, I'll let it go. But I want to say one more thing. You know what I want to say, Cal? The hell with that man; he's never done a thing for either of us." She jammed her foot down on the gas, then looked across at me. "The hell with him, Cal," she said. "You deserve something a whole lot better."

# Chapter 14

"Calvin." Fern passed me in the hall and put something into my hand. It was an envelope with my name on the outside. CALVIN MILLER. I opened it and took out a sheet of paper. PLEASE COME TO MY BIRTHDAY PARTY APRIL 15TH. LOTS OF GOOD FOOD. DANCING. GAMES. NO PRESENTS, PLEASE. JUST YOU. FERN LIGHT.

Why was she inviting me? It was a mistake. I went after her down the hall, but she turned into the math lab, and the bell rang. I ran for my next class. Anyway, I'd see her in Mr. Aketa's room.

"You meant this invitation for Garo, didn't you?" I said later. "I'll give it to him when I get home."

"Garo? Why would you think that? I gave it

to you, didn't I?" Her eyebrows thickened. "So, are you coming?"

"Uhh . . ." I didn't know what to say. Me, go to her party, and not Garo? What sense did that make? "What about Garo?" I asked.

"What about him?"

"Uh, I thought the invitation — "

"I know, I know. You thought it was for him. Are you having a major political crisis over this?"

"You don't want him at your party?" I blurted.

"Did I say that? What are you, his nurse-maid?"

"You're a rough girl," I said.

"I try."

As it turned out, Fern had given Garo an in-vitation, too, but she wasn't a normal person who would just tell me that. She had to put me on the spot. *Are you coming or aren't you? Give me an answer in ten seconds or less!* Probably hoping I'd make a fool of myself, so she could produce another one of her brilliant sarcastic remarks.

Saturday night, Garo spent at least two hours getting ready for Fern's party. First he laid every-thing out, from matching shorts and socks to jacket and vest. Then he showered and brushed his teeth and combed his hair and sprayed him-self with everything available. He changed his tie at least five times, and then at the last minute decided to change his socks and underwear so they'd all match.

"You plan to take your pants down during the party?" I asked.

"Red socks," he said. "Where are my red

socks?'' He finally borrowed a pair from me.

Maybe Mom had thrown his away. Garo didn't like getting rid of his clothes, and Mom was always trying to weed out his old, worn-out stuff. Like she'd weeded out my father? I thought of his blue jacket. How limp it had looked. Even from across the street, even from the other end of the mall, I'd seen that. Maybe he really needed that forty bucks. Maybe he spent all the money he had on coming here. To see me. Maybe he really did come here to see me.

All these things started bouncing around in my brain. And I did something I hadn't done in years, I took Opha Kangaroo off the closet shelf and held her. It was strange. A wave of something like dizziness or sleepiness came over me. I wanted to shut my eyes. I could have dozed off, standing right there.

''What're you doing?'' Garo said, tucking in his shirt.

''Nothing.'' I shoved Opha K. back in the closet.

''You're not even dressed yet, Cal.''

''Maybe I shouldn't go.''

''Shut up and put on a clean shirt. Change your jeans, Cal, they look ready to walk away by themselves.''

I looked down. My jeans were a little grungy.

Garo went into the closet. ''Here, put these on. And then go shave.''

I zipped up the jeans. ''I don't have to shave

tonight. I shaved on Wednesday."

"I shaved," he said.

"You? You did not."

"Sure I did. It's a neat thing to do before a party."

I sniffed him. Sure enough. After-shave lotion. "What did you even have to shave?" I patted his face. "That baby skin?"

I'm not going to relate the whole party. I'm just going to tell the three main things that struck me. The first was the girls making a major fuss over Garo. Every girl there was dressed to kill — heels, makeup, jewelry, hair, clothes. And from the moment we walked into Fern's house, all of them swarmed around Garo.

"He's so so cute," I heard Ami Pelter say. And Margie Clearmount — "He's a little teddy bear. Don't you just want to hug him?"

There were fifteen girls and six boys at the party. The boys were mostly dressed up, too. I was about the only one who looked like nothing special. It didn't bother me until I saw the black girl who had been with Angel and Fern the day they looked in the window of Hair Today. Her name was Iris.

She seemed different from everyone else — I don't mean because she was black. That's too obvious. It was something else about her, maybe the way she carried herself. She had a long neck, and she kind of sailed regally when she walked. She was wearing a short black skirt, some kind of tucked or pleated blouse, silver earrings as big as plates, and black and white zebra stockings.

I couldn't stop looking at her, but I didn't have the nerve to speak to her. I sort of wandered around the outskirts of wherever she was, watching her.

The third main thing about that party was playing Sardines. I never thought I'd hear myself say playing a game like that was memorable. "Since it's my birthday," Fern said, "I get to choose the hider." She looked around the room. "I choose . . . Calvin."

Everyone looked at me. I saw Iris looking at me.

"Get going, Calvin," Fern said. "We'll wait five minutes while you find your hidey hole. Try not to make it too obvious and easy." She shut the lights.

I walked quickly through the dining room and into the front hall. I ran up the stairs. A long dim hall. I opened a door and looked into a bedroom. It might have been her parents'. I backed out and opened another door. Bedroom again. Maybe I could hide in a closet. But that was so obvious. The next door I opened led to the bathroom. I started to back out of there, too, then I heard Fern shouting, "One more minute!" I dashed into the shower stall and pulled the curtain. It was either brilliant or stupid. Either so obvious they'd find me immediately or so obvious it wasn't obvious at all.

I heard footsteps and voices.

"Nobody in here. . . . Maybe he's under the bed. . . . Try the closet. . . . Are your parents going to kill us?"

Someone opened the bathroom door, then closed it. I leaned against the tiles. The door opened again, and a moment later the curtain was pulled back. Hands touched me. "Aha!" someone whispered. Whoever it was got in next to me. "Good place." It was Fern. "But not good enough. I knew you'd do something like this."

How could she know that when I didn't know it myself?

"Because you think you're clever," she whispered, as if I'd asked the question. She was so close I could smell her hair, a lemony scent. "Not talking? Okay. I just wonder, are you shy or just stuck-up?"

What was I supposed to say to that?

"Leslie says you're shy."

What else had Leslie said?

"And that you don't know how to kiss."

My mouth fell open.

"Don't you have anything at all to say?" she whispered.

I thought of something to say! Or *do*. We were alone for another minute, or maybe two minutes. Not more.

Then Candy Perkins found us and climbed in. A moment later, Carl Vazerik was there, and Leslie Branch came right after him. "Oooh, oooh, ooh," Leslie crooned. "What fun. Whose hand is this?'' Someone else got in. It started to get crowded and hot. That was the point of the game. Sardines.

Later, at home, Garo and I talked about the party. He couldn't stop saying what a great time he had, and how pretty Fern looked, and how nice she was to him, and how when he found my hiding place she'd been the one who reached out and hauled him into the shower stall. "I'm just in love with her," he said. He did five push-ups and collapsed on the floor and lay there, smiling.

I could have talked about Iris, how just thinking about her made me feel really peculiar and almost dazed. But I didn't. And there was something else I could have talked about to Garo that I didn't. Something else I didn't want to say. I didn't want to tell him that Fern and I had been kissing in the shower.

# Chapter 15

I saw my father again. This time he was standing across the street from the school and I was in the Language Arts lab. My seat is by the window. We were doing journal writing that day. Mr. Pelter reads our journals once a week, so I never put down anything private. I was trying to write something funny about Mom and the slice of French bread. I got up to stretch and look out the window. Or did I know in some way? Did something tell me to look out? Probably not. Probably I'd looked out that same window in that same way a hundred times before — stood up, stretched, looked out, and sat down without having seen anything worth remembering.

This time, I didn't sit down. I saw my father out there, leaning against a green car and staring across at the school. He was here for me — this time I knew it! Here to see me. Or just to see the place I went to school. He had his hand above his eyes, as if he were keeping out the glare of the sun. But it was a cloudy, gray day.

I left. I walked out of the room. I didn't ask for a pass or anything. I just walked out. I went by Garo's desk. "Hey," he said. I went by Mr. Pelter's desk. "Calvin?" he said.

I closed the door behind me. I walked down the hall, listening to the click and echo of my boots. I went down the stairs. Not thinking, not asking myself why I was doing this or what I was going to say to him. Just moving, as if I was on the end of a rope and something was pulling me forward.

Mrs. Jones-Barbarra stopped me as I was going out the front door. Mr. Pelter must have called down to the office. "What's going on, Calvin?" She took my arm.

"Nothing. Let go of me, please."

"Why did you leave Mr. Pelter's class?"

"No reason. Please let go of me."

"Are you sick?"

"No, I just want to go outside for a minute."

"Calvin. If something's wrong, you can tell me."

"Nothing's wrong. Can I go outside for a minute?"

"This is schooltime, Calvin."

"Just for a minute. Please, it won't be any longer. I'm going to come right back," I said. I tried to move around her.

"You can't get up and walk out of your class, walk out of school on a whim."

"It's not a whim," I said. I yanked my arm free and pushed open the door. The car was gone. My father was gone. There was no sign of him. The whole street was empty. I might have imagined it, imagined the whole thing. Maybe I had.

I got handed two weeks' detention for that, an hour every day after school. And I got lectures, as well, from Mr. Pelter, from Mrs. Jones-Barbarra, from Mom. And from the coach.

"Calvin, I've thought this matter over," he said. "I've given it lots of thought; this is not a hasty decision." He ran his hand over his hair. "In my view, considering this latest stunt, I don't think you should be on the basketball team right now."

What did walking out of Language Arts have to do with basketball?

"Any time you get an idea in your head, you act on it. You do what you want to do. The game starts and you're not there. Now this! It isn't just my judgment, you know. Your teachers concur."

I looked down at my sneakers. My teachers concurred? That really made me feel lousy.

"Calvin, I'm sorry about this. You're a nice guy, but you need some discipline. I hope this doesn't discourage you. You can try out again next term, in the fall. . . . Do you want to say anything?"

I shook my head. What was the point? I could have defended myself, but I didn't want to discuss my father with him or anyone else. That was private.

I found out where my father was staying by calling all the motels in the area and asking for Cameron Miller. It didn't even take as long as it took Tom to get one picture of me and Garo right. I tracked down my father that same day and called before I lost my nerve. He was out.

The next time I called, there was still no answer. I sat down on Alan's bed. Then Garo came to the door. He and Mom had just come back from the dentist. I motioned Garo in. "I'm calling my father."

He sat down next to me. "Good. . . . How was detention?"

I shrugged. "You're supposed to do homework. I read the whole time. Nobody bothers you if they think you're reading something serious." I'd picked up a book called *Woman Warrior* in the library. I thought it was science fiction, but it turned out to be about Chinese people coming to this country, and all the problems they had. It was interesting, because the author made it personal and told a lot of stories about herself and her family.

"How was Dr. Fried?" I dialed the motel again.

"I got three new jokes from him." Garo slapped his face. "I'm still numb on this side."

The phone rang. "Hold on, please," a woman said. Then a moment later, "Red Line Budget Motel."

"Mr. Miller in Room 105."

"One moment, please."

Two more short buzzes. "Hello."

"Hello," I said.

"Hello? Somebody there?"

"Is this — " I started coughing. My throat was dry. "This is Calvin Miller," I said. "Is this Cameron Miller?"

"Calvin?"

"Yes."

"Where are you?"

"I'm home."

"I'd like to see you. This is Calvin, my son, isn't it?"

"Yes."

"Okay. I want to see you. Only I don't think your mother is too happy about the idea."

"You can see me," I said. And I had this mental flash, like a weird vision, of me up on a movie screen, a huge blue-jeaned and booted Calvin, hands on hips like some old fifties cowboy, looming over a tiny dark room where my father sat slumped back, gazing up at the screen.

"Do you want to meet someplace?" he said.

"Where?" I said.

"Wherever you want. Choose a place."

I thought of Le Bread and Buttery. No. The mall. No. "I could come to the motel," I said.

"Do you know where it is?"

"I'll find it."

After I got out of detention the next day, Garo and I caught a bus and went downtown. The motel was on the edge of the downtown area, on East Henry Street. Just a block further south, there were a lot of boarded-up stores and empty warehouses. The motel was a yellow building with a big signboard in front. WELCOME MARY AND MARK ON YOUR TWENTY-FIFTH ANNIVERSARY.

We walked into a small lobby, with a few chairs scattered around, and on a table in a corner a glass coffeepot and a stack of Styrofoam cups. The woman at the registration desk looked up, then went back to reading a newspaper.

"This way," Garo said, pointing to a corridor.

"How do you know?" I felt a little sick. I'd eaten pizza for lunch, which ordinarily I didn't eat, especially at school. I hoped I wouldn't do anything stupid like throw up.

"105 is the first floor." Garo tugged at my sleeve. "Come on. It says so, right there." On the wall an arrow pointed to the numbers 100–120.

"I can't." I was starting to shake inside. In the back of my mind, I'd had this idea that I would stride into my father's room, shake his hand, and say, "Hello, Cameron!" in a forthright, forceful way.

*How're you doing, Cameron? Where have you been? How come you never came here before? What brought you here now?*

I'd ask all these questions that had been on my mind, but at the same time act as if I didn't really care about the answers. I just wanted him to account for himself. Just a point of information.

"Wait," I said. "Wait." I was shaking.

"Want me to do it? I'll tell him you're here."

"He doesn't know you."

"I'll introduce myself." Garo was completely calm. He walked toward the room, then came back and patted my arm. "Sit down, Cal, take a load off. I'll be right back."

I leaned against the wall and watched Garo walk down the corridor. He stopped in front of a door and knocked. The door opened. I couldn't believe how fast it happened. Time seemed to have gone crazy. Garo was turning, looking at me, raising his hand. He called me. "Cal. Come on."

At that moment, I could have walked out. I thought of it. I didn't have to stay there. I didn't have to see my father. I didn't have to do anything. But I went forward. I walked toward Garo in the corridor and my father hidden in the room.

# Chapter 16

My father was standing in the doorway, and he looked so small to me. He was wearing an Elvis T-shirt and tan pants and shoes with no socks on. He looked like he had almost no shoulders at all. "Come on in," he said.

"Hello," I said. It was all backwards, and that was the way I felt — backwards, nervous, confused, nauseous. A light in the room behind him glared into my eyes.

Garo gave me a little shove, and I stumbled into the room. I saw my father's blue jacket hanging over the back of the chair. Big padded shoulders.

We didn't shake hands. We didn't touch. We didn't do anything. Just looked at each other. "Sit down," he said.

I didn't say anything. He looked unhappy,

that's all I could think. He had an unhappy face. He wasn't smiling to see me.

"Sit down," he said again. He looked around the room, pushed a chair forward. He said, "Sit down, young man," to Garo. "So you two are friends," he said.

Garo sat down.

I kept staring at my father, wondering if I looked like him. He had a narrow face, a long nose, a little wisp of a mustache under that nose. "You want a drink?" he said.

And Garo said, "A drink?" in this dumb, shocked voice. It made me want to laugh.

My father bent down to a little refrigerator and took out a bottle of soda — ginger ale, I think, or maybe it was 7-Up, something like that. And he glanced at me and peaked up his eyebrows, as if the two of us understood each other.

"I'll have a drink," I said. I felt better after I said that. Some of my nervousness left me. I don't know why. I walked over to the window and looked out into the parking lot. I looked for his car, the green car I'd seen outside of school. "Where's your car?" I said.

"Oh, ay, ah, I don't have it with me," he said.

"You don't have your car?"

"I, ah, just rented one," he said.

"Just rented one?" Why was I repeating everything he said?

"I came here by bus, then, uh, I rented the car. My car isn't good for a long trip. It burns oil, and . . ." His voice trailed off.

"You followed me," I said.

"What?"

"Did you rent it so you could kidnap me?" I said.

He was squatting on the floor in front of the little refrigerator, still holding the bottle of soda. He started smiling. "Kidnap you? Why would I do that?"

Again I felt confused and stupid, and almost ashamed, as if I'd said something awful.

"I'm not a kidnapper," he said.

I sat down on a chair, but I got up immediately. My father poured soda into two plastic glasses and handed one to each of us. "Thank you," Garo said.

"What were you doing in the mall?" I said.

He looked uncomfortable. "In the mall?"

"I saw you there," I said. "Garo and I were shopping." I suddenly wondered if he'd think that was sissy stuff. "Garo and I were there, and you were there," I said.

"I did follow you," he said. "That, that day, I did follow you. I was parked down the street where you lived and I, I watched you. I saw you outside that day."

He spoke so hesitantly I wondered how he could ever sell anything to anybody. He didn't seem at all like the forceful salesman kind of personality, like the kind of man people were always making jokes about. Would you buy a used car from this man?

Yes! I would! He seemed honest and sincere . . . and weak. I felt sorry for him and, and something . . . something else . . . something hard and tight in my belly, a ball, a wad, like there was a wad of lumpy chewing gum sticking up my guts.

"I saw you raking the yard that day," he said. "I, uh, I saw you, and I saw your mother . . . and then, you know, when you went to the mall, I followed you. Yeh, I followed you."

"How about the movies?" I said. "Did you follow me there, too?"

"Movies?" he said. "What movies?"

"I saw you there, too," I said. "Across the street." But then I wasn't sure. Had it been him? A man in a blue jacket. I wasn't sure. "You were outside my school."

"Yeh, yeh." He nodded. Then he said, "Excuse me." He went into the bathroom, closed the door. You could hear the sounds, you could hear everything in that little room. The toilet flushed. The water ran in the sink, and he came out. His eyes were red, sore-looking. Had he been crying?

"So how do you do in school?" he said.

"Okay," I said.

"He's good," Garo said. My father looked at him. "Cal's a star in Language Arts," he said.

"Is that right?" My father sat down on the edge of the bed.

"No," I said.

"Yeah, he is," Garo said. "Don't listen to him, Mr. Miller. He's always putting himself down." Garo had been sitting in that chair without moving. Now he bounced up, sat down, bounced up again. "Cal's smart," he said. "He's on the basketball team."

"No, I'm not."

"You were."

"I got kicked off," I said.

My father nodded, as if he understood. What could he understand? He didn't know anything about it. Maybe what he understood was how it felt to be kicked off something, kicked out, not wanted.

"Cal's a good writer, too," Garo said. "He reads everything. He's really smart, Mr. Miller."

My father looked at me with a little smile. His mustache crinkled. "Is that right? You like to read?"

I nodded.

"I do, too," he said, almost shyly. He gestured to a pile of books on the little table between the two beds. "You know what I did when I got here? I went to the library and got a card."

He put his hands in his pockets, patted them, then went to the bureau, opened the top drawer and then the next drawer. "Where'd I put it?" He picked up his jacket. "Here," he said, "look at this." He took out a white plastic card. "Temporary library card. They couldn't give me a permanent one because I don't have an address here. But I showed them my card from home, and they gave me this. It's good for a month."

I didn't say anything. He put the card away.

"Where do you live?" I asked.

"Vermont."

"That's where you live?"

"Burlington, Vermont."

"I thought you lived in Maine."

"No. Burlington, Vermont. You ever been there, Cal?" I shook my head. "It's beautiful country," he said. "Right on the lake. Lake Champlain. Beautiful country."

"You sent me a postcard from Maine."

"I did? When was that?"

*When was that?* Didn't he know? Three postcards in nine years, and he couldn't remember sending them? "It was three years ago," I said. And then I repeated it. "Three years ago!" Maybe I shouted. I could sense Garo going rigid in his chair. I felt stupid again, ashamed again.

"Oh . . . I was on vacation, I guess," my father said in a low voice.

I wanted him to speak up, I wanted him to shout at me. I wanted him to say something, ask me something, demand something, tell me something. I wanted him to tell me *something*, but I didn't know what it was.

"Want some more soda?" he asked.

"No." In my head I was shouting again. *I don't want more soda. No, I don't want more soda! No!* I hit the table and the little plastic cup tipped over. The soda went all over the floor.

We all looked at it. My father said, "I know . . . I know I haven't been a very good . . . I haven't been a good father. It's . . . it's hard, I should have, I should have done a lot of things and I didn't . . . I didn't do a lot of things. . . . I just didn't. Do. A lot of things."

115

I went into the bathroom and came back with tissues to wipe up the soda.

"You don't have to do that," my father said.

"It's all right." I threw the tissues in the wastebasket.

"So you like to read?" he said. "That's great! What kind of books do you like to read?"

"Science fiction," I said. "Different things. I like to read about other people, I guess . . . like other worlds."

"You do?" he said. "That's great!" He reached over and patted my knee. And he said, "You're a fine boy, Cal. You're a fine boy. I came here to see you, to see who you are. I knew you'd be someone I could be proud of. And I was right. I'm proud of you."

I felt mad . . . scared. . . . Some half-crazy feeling grabbed me like hands. I didn't know what it was. I heard someone making hard gaspy noises, and then I knew it was me, and I was crying.

# Chapter 17

"Where's your little curly headed friend?" Fern said, getting in line behind me in the cafeteria.

"Garo's sick. Flu or something." The whole house had been in an uproar since last night when Alan came home with four surprise guests, including the Perfect Person, Diane. I'd expected her to be a blonde movie star, bimbo type. Surprise. She was wearing jeans, granny glasses, and her hair was brown. And she was probably as old as Mom.

Mom sent me out to buy food. When I came back, she was making beds and cleaning up the attic bathroom and my room. She was giving that to Diane and the two other women. The other man was going to sleep in the living room.

Then, as if that wasn't enough, in the middle of the night, Garo woke up sick. He was throwing up, and Mom got up and took care of him.

"Poor little Curly," Fern said. "Give him my regards."

I could never tell with Fern if she was serious or mocking. "Where's your shadow?" I asked.

"You mean Angel? She's no shadow. There's more to her than that."

"If you say so."

"I do. Watch out for those glib guesses." She came closer, stood right next to me. I thought of the shower. What if she wanted to kiss right here?

"You're a funny one," Fern said. "You never smile."

I pulled up my lips, put my hands to either side of my mouth, and stretched.

"Well, you look a lot better that way," she said. "You ought to practice. Take some lessons from Curly. He smiles enough for five of you."

"You have an opinion about everything, don't you?" I said.

"Sure," she said. "Why not, don't you?"

"I keep my opinions to myself."

"Why would you want to do that? Are they so precious you can't share them?"

I grunted.

"Oh, that's eloquent," she said. "Uggh! Uggh! Me, Tarzan, or something brilliant like that."

I took a tray and glanced ahead. Why was this line moving so slowly? How long was I going to have to listen to Fern work me over?

"Don't you like people to say what they think?" she asked.

I grunted again. She kicked my foot. "Shoot! That hurt, Fern. Why'd you do that?"

"Just want to see if you have any human responses. Are you aware, Calvin, that you grunt? *Uggha ugggha uggha*," she said in a deep voice. "That's ugly. I'm serious now. I'm doing you an excellent favor telling you this. I want you to work on your personality profile."

I rubbed my ankle. "I'm honored by your interest."

"You should be. I don't waste my time on most people."

I put a tuna fish sandwich on my tray.

"Unfortunate choice," Fern said. "The tuna is always soggy. Too much mayonnaise. Cheese is a far better option."

"I hate cheese," I said. "The cheese here is the worst I've ever tasted. It tastes like plastic and sticks to your teeth like chewing gum." How was that for an opinion?

When I took out my wallet to pay, the paper with my father's address fell out. I glanced at it. He lived on Isham Street in Burlington. "Just a couple of rooms," he'd said. He lived alone. He had given me his address so we could stay in touch.

"Stay in touch?" Mom said when I told her. "Cameron Miller stay in touch? That'll be the day!" And she reached out, the way she always did, as if she were going to pinch or lightly slap my cheek.

I stepped back. "Don't. I'm too old for that stuff, Mom."

"Sorry," she said.

And then I felt sorry, as if I'd hurt her.

I walked to the back of the cafeteria where I usually sat. Fern sat down across from me. "Don't you usually brown bag it?" she asked.

How'd she know that? I bit into the sandwich. "Good tuna. Excellent sogginess."

"I usually brown bag it, too, except when I forget to make my lunch or get too busy and have to buy it, like today."

"My mother didn't have time to make my lunch this morning, either," I said.

"Your mother makes your lunch?" Fern paused with her sandwich halfway to her mouth. "What a difficult life you must have, Calvin. Does she make your bed, too?"

"What's so terrible about that?"

"Oh, and I suppose she brushes your teeth for you, also."

"What about your friend Iris?"

"Why her, all of a sudden? You think she has a servant? I know for a fact that she makes her own lunch. She's no parasite. Her mother's a lawyer and doesn't have time to stand around slathering peanut butter on bread."

"Is she the type who says what she thinks, too?"

"Iris's mom? What do you think! You don't get to be a lawyer by hiding under the sofa."

"I meant Iris," I said. "Your friend." The longer I talked to Fern the less I could believe we'd actually pressed close to each other and kissed. It seemed like something I must have made up in a dream.

"Well, she's more tactful than I am," Fern said. "But that's how she got her boyfriend."

"Her boyfriend?"

"Yes, her boyfriend. That's what I said. Her boyfriend. His name is Sidney, Sidney Greene. She went up to him the first day she met him, she put her hand on his shoulder, and she said, 'You know, I think you're a very fine person.' Because she'd seen him do something nice for someone else, and she thinks people ought to be told when they do something good. She believes in appreciating people."

"Where do you know her from? She doesn't go to our school, does she?"

"No, she goes to Smith. We were down at the Y together; we took a class there. We were eyeing each other — I guess it was a mutual attraction. And then when I found out her name was Iris and she found out mine was Fern, that was it. We knew we had to be friends."

"Swimming class?" I said.

"What? Oh. No, CPR."

"CPR?"

"Surely, you know what that is, Calvin?"

I did, but I was thinking about Iris having a boyfriend. Well, what had I expected? By the time Iris crowded into the shower, everyone was screaming, "Sardines! Sardines!" She was almost the last one in. I couldn't even get near her. She was laughing; everyone was laughing and squeezing in together. It was dark. Iris couldn't tell me from anyone else in that mob. And when we got out, well, I didn't do anything to get to know her. I never even spoke to her. I had felt too self-conscious. What Fern would probably call my fatal flaw.

"I like her," I said suddenly.

"That shows good taste, anyway," Fern said. "Maybe there's some hope for you." She looked at me over her container of milk. "You like her? You really do?" She gave me a little smile.

Was that actually approval?

"Hang in there, Calvin," she said. "You never know what could happen."

# Chapter 18

My father called me. "Hello, son," he said.

"Hello — " I couldn't get out the D word. *Dad.*

"Well, I just called to say hello, Cal. I'm home now."

"Okay."

"You doing okay?"

"Yeah, sure." I cleared my throat. "Uh, I forgot to ask you. What do you do?"

"Do?"

"I mean, work."

"Oh. I'm a salesman."

"What do you sell?"

He laughed. "Shoes, underwear, paper goods, whatever."

Then there was a silence. He broke it. "Well, I won't keep you. I just wanted to say hello."

"That's all right."

"I like to hear your voice."

"Oh. Okay. Cool."

"How's the schoolwork?"

"Good."

"Anything I can do for you?"

"Uhh — " Like what? "No," I said. "Thanks."

"Well, you let me know if there's anything I can do for you."

"Okay."

"I'll just say good-bye then."

"Good-bye." I started to hang up, then I heard him still talking.

". . . call you again," he was saying. And then we did hang up.

Just before spring break, our class had a picnic at Enoch Falls Park. It was a school tradition, once in the spring and once in the fall. Mr. Aketa and Mr. Herrick chaperoned. We had a cold clear day. The sky was blue, and a wind rustled the pines. As soon as we got off the bus, we unloaded the food — bagloads of sandwiches, boxes of soda, and a crate of potato chips.

We ate and then we played Frisbee and softball, even though there were still pockets of snow among the rocks. Some of the kids took off their shoes and went wading in the pool below the falls. "Freezing," they screamed.

Before the sun got too low, Mr. Aketa organized everyone for a class picture. He had a Nikon camera on a tripod. "Kids, line up by height, tallest in back." Everyone milled around. "Come on," Mr. Aketa pleaded, "let's have a little initiative here. A little cooperation. Kids! My baby, Karin, is more cooperative than this." Instead of a boy, the Kenneth Mason Aketa he'd expected, he'd had a girl, Karin Mason Aketa.

I knelt down in front near Garo. "Get back in line, Calvin," Mr. Aketa said. "You're too tall for the front line."

Someone put their hands on my head and climbed on my shoulders. I say *someone*, but it was Leslie the witch. "Stand up," she ordered.

"What? Get off me!" But I really liked it.

"Move to the back, Calvin," she said, "Come on, you heard Mr. Aketa. Stand up. We're the tallest now."

"Good!" Mr. Aketa said. "That looks good, Leslie and Cal. This'll make the picture."

I locked my arms around Leslie's knees. "Don't drop me," she said in my ear.

"Okay, smiles now, everyone," Mr. Aketa said. "Say cheese, kids. Think of rat's teeth and smelly socks."

Leslie kept fooling around, putting her hands over my ears and my eyes, or grabbing me by the hair. I was going to dump her when Mr. Aketa was done, but then Kenny Fisher was there, with Laurel Salmon on his shoulders.

"Let's have a race," Kenny said. "Miller and Branch against Salmon and Fisher."

"A race, a race," Leslie cried in that squeaky voice of hers.

"Wait . . . us, too," I heard Garo say. He galloped up with Fern on his shoulders, or maybe I should say staggered.

"Oh, now everybody's doing it," Leslie said.

"Goodness, Leslie, my apologies!" Fern said. "I didn't realize it was an original patented idea."

Everyone *was* doing it. The guys were kneeling down. The girls were climbing on their shoulders. Someone marked out a course and someone else got Mr. Herrick to drop the flag (a T-shirt on a stick) for the start.

"And they're off!" Mr. Herrick yelled, like an announcer at the horse races.

Leslie beat her hands on my shoulders in a frenzy, as if I really were a horse. "Go, Cal, go! Go, go, go!"

I ran all out. I got caught up in it. I wanted to win, and what flashed through my mind was this: *I'll tell my father.* As if winning a dumb race like this meant something.

We did it. We won. We came in first. Leslie bent over me, her arms draped around my neck. "Fantastic! You were wonderful," she said. And right there, in front of everyone, she kissed me.

# Chapter 19

"Do you think I should go see my father?" I asked Mom.

"Maybe. Do you think it would be any good?"

"I don't know. Every time he calls, we don't have anything to say to each other."

"Well, that should answer your question. You'll go all the way up there, spend all that money, and the two of you won't say three words to each other."

I don't know why, but I kept thinking about visiting him. One weekend when Alan was home, I talked to him about it. I don't know why I did that, either. I'd never talked to Alan about anything before. "So what do you think?" I said, already feeling I was wasting his time, and boring him, besides.

He steepled his fingers and did his Alan rumble. "What do I think? I think, Calvin . . ." He looked out the window. "I think, Calvin, you probably should go to see him."

"Why?" My head always got hot when I talked about my father, and I got that chewing gum lump in my stomach.

"Why? Why? He's your father. That's why."

"Is that a good enough reason?"

What did it even mean that he was my father? He could have been someone off the street for all I knew about him.

"Alan, you're more my father than he is," I said.

"Well, thank you for that." Alan rubbed my back. 'I'm fond of you, too, Cal." He hugged me, got me in a bear embrace. I thought he might kiss me, but he didn't.

He wiped his eyes. "Calvin, I don't know if reason has too much to do with this kind of thing. For better or worse, the man is your father. See what I mean?"

"I guess so," I said.

"No, that's it," he said. "That's the bottom line."

My father called again. Another awkward phone call. They didn't seem to get any better.

I tried to write to him. But I didn't know what to say. Even if I sent him a letter, he wouldn't answer me. Maybe in three years he'd send me a postcard.

* * *

128

Sometimes I forgot all about my father.

Sometimes I thought about him more than ever.

Sometimes I wished he had never come to see me and that I could just clear my mind of him and never think about him again.

"Hey, watch those kidneys!" I said. I had a neck hold on Garo, and he was rabbit-punching me. We wrestled across the room and banged into the desk.

"Garo! Cal! What are you two boys doing?" Mom called. "The ceiling is going to fall!"

We paused. We were both panting. "Are we doing anything, Garo?"

"No, Cal, we're not doing anything. You want another kidney punch?"

"No, Garo. Nice of you to offer." I jerked his head a little bit, then let him go.

"I've got a new joke," he said, getting out his notebook. "There was this man who had a dog who liked to play checkers. They go into a bar one day —"

"Do you think I should visit my father?"

"Don't you want to hear the rest of my dog joke?"

"Not now." I jumped up restlessly.

"Why don't you just start out with a phone call to your father?" Garo asked. "I mean, you call him for a change."

"Why?"

"Because he's always calling you. But if you

129

want to go visit him, you should do it. You've been agonizing over it long enough. I'll go with you," he added.

"You don't have to do that."

"I know that," he said. "But you might want company on a trip like that. You know . . ."

I put my hand on his shoulder. "Garo, you're a good friend. You're probably the greatest friend."

He shrugged. "I know that, too. . . . Anyway, so are you."

"You're sure I should do this?" I asked Garo.

He nodded, and I dialed. The phone rang in my father's apartment. "Hello?" he said.

"It's me, uh, Calvin."

"Well. Hello."

"Hello."

There was a silence. What did we have to say to each other? Nothing. What did we have in common? Nothing.

I cleared my throat. "Just called to say hello."

"That's very nice of you, Calvin."

I cleared my throat again. "This is the first time I've called you."

"That's right! I knew it was going to be you. I was reading that book you told me about, and the phone rang, and I thought, it's going to be Calvin."

"Oh."

"Yeah," he said.

We stumbled along for a few minutes about

the book he was reading and the movie I'd seen and a TV show we'd both hated.

"Well . . . I guess I'll call you again sometime," I said.

"Okay, I hope you do," he said.

"If that's all right with you," I said.

"Oh, sure," he said. "It's fine with me. Yes. I like it."

"So, okay. Good-bye, uh — "

"Good-bye, son. You take care now."

"Okay."

"You be good to yourself, son."

"I will," I said.

"Good. All right, then, I'm going to let you go."

"Good-bye," I said.

"Good-bye."

"Okay," I said. "You take care, too."

"I will." He seemed to be waiting, waiting for me to say something else.

I leaned forward. "So I'm going to hang up now." But I didn't. Say it, I thought. You can say it. My hands were sweaty. And then I said it. "Good-bye, Dad," I said, and I put down the phone.

# About the Author

NORMA FOX MAZER is the author of more than nineteen books for young readers, among them *Taking Terri Meuller, When We First Met, Three Sisters,* and the Newbery Honor *After the Rain.* Ms. Mazer has twice received the Lewis Carroll Shelf Award, has won the Edgar Award and the California Young Reader Medal, and has been nominated for the National Book Award.

*C, My Name Is Cal* is a companion book to *A, My Name Is Ami; B, My Name Is Bunny; D, My Name Is Danita;* and *E, My Name Is Emily,* all recently published by Scholastic.

Ms. Mazer lives with her husband, Harry Mazer, in the Pompey Hills, outside Syracuse, New York.

## The best stories about best friends!

### More books by
# NORMA FOX MAZER

**Apple® Paperbacks**

❑ NU43896-4 **A, My Name Is Ami** $2.95

❑ NU43895-6 **B, My Name Is Bunny** $2.95

❑ NU41832-7 **C, My Name Is Cal** $2.95

**Books for older readers**

❑ NU43817-4 **Three Sisters** $2.95

❑ NU43823-9 **When We First Met** $2.95

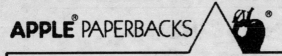

# THE BABY-SITTERS CLUB®

### by Ann M. Martin

Collect Them All!

The seven girls at Stoneybrook Middle School get into all kinds of adventures...with school, boys, and, of course, baby-sitting!

# **APPLE** PAPERBACKS

# THE GYMNASTS™

### by Elizabeth Levy

Available wherever you buy books, or use this order form.

-------------------------------------------------------------

Scholastic Inc., P.O. Box 7502, 2931 East McCarty Street, Jefferson City, MO 65102

Please send me the books I have checked above. I am enclosing $_____ (please add $2.00 to cover shipping and handling). Send check or money order — no cash or C.O.D.s please.

Name _____

Address _____

City _____ State/Zip _____

Please allow four to six weeks for delivery. Offer good in the U.S. only. Sorry, mail orders are not available to residents of Canada. Prices subject to change.

GYM1090